THE HOCKEY FAN CAME RIDING

THE HOCKEY FAN CAME RIDING

Birk Sproxton

For Jan
(pool sharks)
with best wishes
Birk Sproxt
Oct 30/90

Red Deer College Press

The Publishers

Red Deer College Press
56 Avenue and 32 Street Box 5005
Red Deer Alberta Canada T4N 5H5

Credits

Design & typesetting: Boldface Technologies Inc.
Cover art: Scott Barham
Cover design: Jim Brennan
Author photo: Elaine McRoberts
Printed in Canada by Gagné Printing Ltd.

Acknowledgements

The author acknowledges the assistance provided by Alberta Culture and Multiculturalism in the preparation of this book.

Parts of this book have appeared in *Border Crossings, New Quarterly, NeWest Review, Secrets from the Orange Couch,* in the anthology *The Rocket, The Flower, The Hammer, and Me* and have been broadcast on CBC *Alberta Anthology.*

The publishers gratefully acknowledge the financial contributions of the Alberta Foundation for the Literary Arts, Alberta Culture and Multiculturalism, the Canada Council, Red Deer College and Radio 7 CKRD.

Canadian Cataloguing in Publication Data

Sproxton, Birk, 1943-
The Hockey Fan Came Riding
ISBN 0-88995-056-3
I.Title.
PS8587.P76H62 1990 C813'.54 C90-091420-3
PR9199.3.S675H62 1990

For

Lorraine,

Shannon

and

Andrea

When the great fen or moor…is frozen, many young men play upon the ice…some tie bones to their feet and under their heels, and, shoving themselves by a little picked staff, do slide as swiftly as a bird flyeth in the air or an arrow out of a crossbow. Sometimes two run together with poles, and hitting one the other, either one or both do fall, not without hurt; some break their arms, some their legs, but youth, desirous of glory, in this sort exerciseth itself against the time of war.

–John Stow, *A Survey of London* (1598)

The findings of the discredited paleontologist Gardener who claimed that the skate – or shate – was the turning point in the contest for supremacy between *Homo sapiens* and primordial man – have been proven fraudulent – but isn't it true that we enjoy on ice skates a sense of fleetness that seems to be a primordial memory?

–John Cheever, *Oh What a Paradise It Seems* (1982)

"O where are you going?" said reader to rider.

–W.H. Auden (1932)

Contents

Icing the Puck

Of arms and the puck I sing, of the woman behind the screen, how hands and arms and skates and feet and sticks fly down and up the ice, how the long strides and the push of the stretched leg glide up your spine, lift your head to the cool air breezing your throat; of the hockey fan finding the Holy Grail, of hockey night in Leningrad, the warm red wine, what happens at the border crossing, how he uses his head to draw first blood, of northern lights dancing in the sky.

Of the underground hockey game, of bomb shelters and bus rides, of bouncing buttocks and pucks ringing the changes, the lament of the stay-at-home defenceman, *blue, blue the blue lines* he sings, what the coach says after the period, of the thin red line, of blood and song lines, how Gene learns of penalties, what happens when the hockey fan turns on the radio, the leap, leap, leaping of the fish, why he contemplateth religious conversion, of pontoon feet and the prose romance, and the game at the end of the earth over time.

I sing of bombardiers and trucks, of the shiny skin magazine, of scars on the surface, the planes soaring over the North Pole, pontoons and canoes in the warm wet rain, how you give it all you've got to take what you can get, the ice fishing tragedy, of Pin Man and the Fortress of the Czars, the road games in Newfoundland – of these and the puck I sing.

Al go tender
Al go quick
Al jump over the goalie stick
Go Al Go
Go Al Go

Aurora Borealis

This story begins in snow. Light dusty flakes float down on the Laurentian Shield north of the 54th parallel, a setting not as far north as Yellowknife or Inuvik or Tuktoyaktuk, nor as far north as Helsinki or Stockholm or Leningrad on the edge of the Baltic Sea, but inland and surely north from where you now lounge in your chair or lollygag on the bed. In this story a boy lies asleep dreaming of hockey. Every night he dreams of hockey in the Big Rink and wishes he could play night and day and dance on his toes, skate zinging across the lake to the shimmy, shimmy, shimmer of the shifting borealis.

One night as he dreams his hardest she comes into his dream, her hard hat dusted with snow, a fairy godmother with sprightly eyes who sees the boyish dreams and makes a wish for him. She speaks the words:

"Let there be water, frozen for toboggans and skating, children to walk on winter water, wade in the drifts of snow, and in the night let skaters and deft stickhandlers dance the sky with me in a shape-shifting shimmer deke and feint.

"Let there be fire to forge the keen-edged skates, stones to grind them, cows and pigs to donate their hides, and kangaroos too for Pro's and Tacks.

"Let there be thrones of tires, tons of truck, tractor and car tires rolling round and round to the sloughs and lakes and ponds, tires to circle and flames to flicker in the black smoke. Let children huddle around the tires steaming to put on skates, to warm up and thaw out mittens. They will have tears and singed eyelashes.

"Let there be sandwiches frozen and smoked over tire fires, laughter and jokes and stories in the dark night under the trestle where Tom jumped off into a snowdrift (the train was coming) and broke his tooth.

"There should be sweat and hockey smells, the looping slice and swerve of figures, there should be pucks and friction tape, conveyor belts to carpet the floors of arenas and outdoor shacks."

And three times she glides in a glistening figure 8, shining on her golden skates.

"Let there be groping under parkas, fiddling with flies and buttons. There will be bodychecks, rubbing of noses and testing of tongues. Let there be smoke and song and stories to huff and puff into the black night and tickle the stars."

And the words creep softly on tiptoe and wrap him warm in his dreams and she sees they are good.

The Hockey Fan Sets Out

Late in 1984, Boxing Day, the hockey fan prepares to fly with his sons to Europe. Denis and his team have been invited to an international bantam hockey tournament in Helsinki, and Mark, now 17, will travel with the group. The hockey fan runs his eyes over the atlas, fingers the metal globe. They will fly to Helsinki and then cruise from Helsinki to Stockholm where the hockey players will be billeted with Swedish families, and then fly to Leningrad for a cultural tour and one exhibition game, outdoors. The hockey fan rummages through his books on Russian art and history, dreams of the Winter Palace and the Hermitage. He runs his fingers down the itinerary.

Dec 27   *Arrive in Helsinki.*

Dec 29–31   *Hockey Tournament in Tappara (Tampere).*

Jan 1–2   *Hockey in Helsinki, if the team finishes first or second. Celebrate New Year in Helsinki, win or lose.*

Jan 3   *Silja Line to Stockholm. Overnight cruise.*

Jan 4–7   *Stockholm. Exhibition games.*

Jan 7   *Overnight cruise to Helsinki.*

Jan 8   *Helsinki to Leningrad. Finn Air.*

Jan 8–12   *Leningrad. Tour the Hermitage, the Winter Palace, the Peter and Paul Fortress.*

Jan 12   *Leningrad to Helsinki. Overnight in the Hotel Presidentii.*

Jan 13   *Helsinki to Seattle. Bus to Vancouver. Air Canada to Edmonton.*

What the Hockey Fan Sees

For the hockey fan the trauma of travel has bodily consequences. A fierce cold ambushes him in a Tampere bomb shelter and hauls him by the nose and throat to an apoteeki in Helsinki where he buys decongestant tablets. Through bleary eyes and the snuffle and snort of cold he sees again and with new clarity that his playing days are over: he is a fan, too old to be called up to the bigs – too big too. Forty is a weighty number – makes you ponder us and them and thee. Yes, he is a fan, not a player, but he isn't ready to give up. No one who has played ever gives up. Muscle memory they call it. He asks himself: How does a hockey fan play? What comes after play? More play, be/fore play? Word play?

Note Book

1 The word fan is short for fanatic.

2 Your mother quits going to the rink when she learns that hockey can be heard as well as seen.

3 The word puck is not in the Bible.

4 The word rhapsody derives from the Greek *rhapsodeia,* the recitation of selections from epic poetry, related to *rhaptein* to sew and *aiden* to sing; akin to Old High German *worf* or scythe handles. A rhapsody is a miscellaneous collection; a musical composition of irregular form having an improvisatory character. Elevated, rapturous. Make it up as you go, sing and sew, cut a wide swath, lift your spirits: bust into song, belly up, belly up, bust for the net, belly up – bust for the net, a net for the bust, with a big sweep check, belly up, belly up.

5 The professionals know how face-offs work. Sometimes one side has the advantage because the other guys have a penalty. Ref caught him with his hands in somebody else's pants. You can't do that, you horrid, horrid man, you're arrested, you're arrested, off you go, awful thing. So one side is shorthanded. The whistle calls everybody to order; it stops the play and both sides line up for another shift. Some shifts have more than one face-off and some face-offs use more than one shift. The pro's know face-offs are puck droppings; they punctuate the action of the prose; they make you stop, take a breath through the nose and start, again, like semi-colons. Yes, face-offs are semi-colons; you wouldn't want to stumble on one; eyes open, you watch for the droppings. You watch for the verb, for the word; you sniff out the puck. You knows your prose.

The Hockey Fan Seeks the Holy Grail

1   The hockey fan steps off the ramp and onto the tarmac. He stretches his arms to the damp fog of the Baltic night. This is Russia and the night is huge and silent. Lights flicker in the distance. Fluffy flakes of snow drift and swirl. A tall uniformed man with a flashlight sweeps the ground with circles of light and the passengers shuffle around him, staying close to the plane until a chugging motor moves out of the dark. It's a blunt-nosed tractor towing a squared-off caboose. The windows of the tractor are slanted and flat like a World War II Jeep. The uniformed man walks to the trailer and with swinging arcs of his flashlight waves people aboard.

Wooden benches line the caboose walls, steel bars strike dark lines against the frosted windows. "A cattle car," says someone in the corner. "Mooooo," calls another voice from another corner. People nudge into seats or grab the cold steel. The lights go out ("a black-out, a bombing raid," say the voices) and the car rumbles over the tarmac.

The hockey fan walks into the foyer. He narrows his eyes against the sudden light, tries to find his balance. Coloured mosaic tile on the floor. A wall covered with photos. Lenin leans into a crowd with arms outstretched. Lenin with a group of students, Lenin signs documents, rewrites the world. A family portrait, fixed, pinned there firm on the wall. This is Lenin's city. Men and women in uniforms, khaki or blue (the police from *Gorky Park?*) walk by, indifferent. At the other end of the foyer are three stalls for visa inspection and the passengers break into eddies of purse-shuffling and wallet-searching. The lines lurch forward to the stamping fist, the searching eye, the head nodding people through.

They enter another holding pen and approach another man in uniform standing beside an x-ray machine. The hockey fan lists his possessions on a piece of brown newsprint. A tiny page. Do you list eyeglasses? Wallet? This pencil?

At the x-ray chute the man scrutinizes the form, a magic marker in his hand. The guts of suitcases become a tumble of socks and underwear in the x-ray window.

"Any books, magazines, firearms, drugs?"

Siberia, a local jail, the gulag, the long swim to Helsinki. The hockey fan imagines a life of crime, enters a silent movie of lust and hankering: deep kisses, dry wines. Pickerel cheeks, wild rice. Warm fleshy curves and chocolate-covered almonds, a neat smash of Johnny Walker Black Label, fingertips fluttering down the spine, wet lips, a deep sigh. The x-ray man rummages through the carry-on and draws a tight line around the scribbles on the page, circles the notes and numbers of dollars, crowns, Finn marks. *O* the small *o* of expelled breath.

He's in. And begins to wait, upstairs. Another line, another cage, another uniform, a woman. How many dollars in a ruble? Canadian?

Outside the bar there is no bartender. Wait again, a TV basketball game. Three quick passes and the ball arcs above the fluid movement of the big men jumping, arms extended into spiky fingers. He sees the stoniness of the stone, the ball in the basket, the basket in the ball. And he waits.

The Hotel Pulkovskaya, only a few minutes in a diesel-smelling bus from the airport, is home base now, a block of white stone and glass framed in the shape of a huge H. A corridor on the second floor connects front and rear sections, links the upright pillars of the H. In the foyer a snowman smiles cheerfully. Beside the elevators, women shift papers across a table. Down the long corridor to a nightclub in the front block. Booths with curved seats and soft lights.

The first supper. Beef tongue/borscht/dark rye bread/tea, hot tea/caviar/potatoes. Cabbage. Beets. "Think we'll ever get bacon and eggs?" Danish. Pepsi, vodka, brandy. Cognac, cognac, cognac.

2   The hockey fan hums to himself as he walks along the Moscow Prospect, hands tucked into the pockets of his big arctic parka. He loves the bite of Baltic air, the blue and yellow signs marking the subway stations, the sculptures and statues, the human scale of five-storey buildings. This is Leningrad, an intentional city Dostoevsky called it, and today as he walks near the hotel, the hockey fan has his intentions. Today he plans to test the economic system. Wednesday he goes to the hockey game, Thursday to the ballet, but today he goes shopping.

He strikes across the street at a traffic circle near the hotel. In the centre a huge sculpture dedicated to the war dead stretches blue-grey steel fingers to the flakes of snow. Underground, beneath the sculpture, in the entrance to the subway is a photograph gallery. A woman pulls her sleigh, her child, dead, wrapped in a tattered blanket. In this gallery all is tidy. Rectangles and glass frame the broken buildings, the shattered windows. The hockey fan clutches Finnish and Swedish bills in his pocket, Canadian dollars, the rubles he bought at the airport.

Surfacing, he walks into the department store, a squat rectangle of grey concrete slabs and grey aluminum windows. Inside, lineups for trinkets, souvenirs, linens. The hockey fan drifts around. Glassware twinkles at him, catches his eye. He steps into line behind six women who shuffle and mumble. They move forward slowly, shaking their babushka'd heads.

He points to a twinkly goblet. The clerk puts it on the counter top and rings it with her pencil. He likes the goblet, its heft, the fine balance; it winks at him. On the bottom, a sticker says ten rubles. The clerk taps her pencil on the counter. He will use his finest English. "Excuse me, my dear, my lovely dove, my honey bunch, I want the goblet, I will pay cash money, rubles and kopeks. And why don't you smile dearest chuck."

She holds up one finger, talks to him. Yes, he nods and reaches for the goblet, but she jerks it back and returns it to the shelf. She raises her voice, her eyebrows bristle. Stupid Kanadienski tourist she is saying, your mother wears army boots, your head is thick as stone. She thunks her pencil on the counter, complains to herself.

The hockey fan begins to see. He makes a great leap forward, an intellectual leap. It's all done with paper. Peter the Great said let there be a city and architects drew up sketches and designed great buildings. He intended that a city should be built and it was. In this city Lenin and Shklovsky wrote papers. Leningrad is a city of paperwork – the city depends on swapping paper. Steam in with a ship, get some paper, chuff away into the Baltic Sea. Drive a truck over the ice, get a piece of paper, chug away into the winter mist.

Yes, Hitler too tried to make a deal with the Russians. He offered bombs and kept papers ready in reserve for his generals. They were to meet in Leningrad, at St. Isaac's Cathedral. Had invitations printed on fine linen with only the date to be added later/sooner. They laid siege to the city and for nine hundred days sent messages of thumping death. Boom, they said, take that and crash, take that. Tried to tear the city, shred the people. Roll them into little spit balls. Blow their house down. You can see pock marks in the columns of St. Isaac's. But the people stuck out their chinny chin chins and Hitler's invitations sat in the vault with the other papers, waiting.

Now the hockey fan stands in a department store lineup, waiting for his paper. "One," he says, holding up a finger. The clerk heaves her shoulders, writes on a slice of brown newsprint. He takes the paper to the cashier, then returns with two slices for the scowling one. She plunks the goblet down, rings it with her pencil, a fine authentic ring. He smiles a big smile, the goblet winks and smiles back at him.

She waits for him to move. He stands there, motions with his hands, smiling. She shakes her head. "Sure, you don't carry unwrapped crystal halfway around the world," he tells her.

He tucks the Grail into his parka pocket. "Danke, merci, kitos," he says, "thank you, my sweetheart, my honey bunch, my darling," skips out into the crisp air, spins down the sidewalk, fingers clutching the Grail.

3 Bus trips unfold a kaleidoscope of city images: the statue of Pushkin, ice cream vendors on street corners, lineups, women pushing snow shovels, courtyards inside apartment blocks, the Pravda building on the edge of the canal. The Peter and Paul Fortress, burial place of the czars. He shoulders around the building, stomps his feet. Across the river, January 1905, workers marched stomping to the Winter Palace to give the Czar a petition. More than one thousand killed that day. Bloody Sunday they call it: they wanted to give the Czar a paper. Near the Admiralty Building, a horseman on a saddle of snow rides upward and upward, going nowhere in a parchment sky. The Hermitage with Picasso, Matisse, Rembrandt. Twenty-five Rembrandts, Michaelangelo, room after room, canvas after canvas, a thousand rooms quick-paced, up and down and around, galloping through the Impressionist section. To St. Isaac's again, the religious icons and images lovingly restored. A pendulum attached to the highest dome, up one hundred metres, they say, shows how the earth rotates on its axis. Fur hats mill around and babushka'd babas at their posts scold visitors who touch the brass, the marble, jade, lapis lazuli, the polished wood, glass display cases in museums and shops. And Beriozka shops.

Westerners always go Beriozka shopping. The goodies are laid out within reach in the Western tradition. You touch and caress and pay in foreign currency, preferably U.S. dollars. Liqueurs and vodka, postcards, hand-painted nesting dolls with smiling faces – even the tiniest of them has blushing red dots on her cheeks – and books on art, economics, history, philosophy. Cognac. The hockey fan fondles his doll, a little doll he can call his own, and noses through books. *On The Dictatorship of the Proletariat*. A hardcover with paper dust jacket, 585 pages, photos of Marx and Lenin, all for one ruble and 50 kopeks says the sticker, a "Beriozka" across the top of the large BS on the logo. He steps forward clutching his Lenin and his doll. The woman at the counter smiles at him.

She offers Swedish crowns for change, but the hockey fan wants Finn marks. He will spend money in the bar of the Hotel Presidentii or in a nightclub dancing with beautiful Finnish women. They will laugh and flirt with him, their voices bell-like, ringing with pleasure. The blonde one will take his hand and lead him to her apartment. He will have his book tucked under his arm. They will lie on the bed and slowly turn the pages, leaf by leaf. She will cuddle up to him to read the book, they will turn the pages making eyes at each other. She will hold the wine goblet to his lips, he will hold it to hers. They will spread the covers and read each other, make music together.

He hums to himself in the diesel fumes of the bus, he floats down the Moscow Prospect. In the sauna her breasts shine, water drips from her golden hair. She holds the goblet in her fingertips, she reaches through the steam and touches his cheek.

He glides into the hotel foyer, book in hand, dolls nesting in his pocket. Denis, coughing, tugs on his sleeve, says they have a throat spray in the hotel boutique. The hockey fan salutes the woman at the counter. She does not speak English. The music of her voice makes him think of towels and dripping hair. He coughs, he opens his mouth. In a series of gestures he sprays his throat.

She hands him a box littered with blue and white letters and numbers. How often should this stuff be used? She answers in Russian. The hockey fan shifts his weight, he feels steam on his cheek. Combien de fois par jour? "Aah," she says and starts to slice the air with her hand, bending at the waist. Un, deux....

He pays close attention. She is a handsome woman, wool sweater and skirt. He ignores the rows and rows of goblets behind her. He ignores the three-ruble price stickers. He steps back. Thinks of Lenin, clutches his book, thinks of the Grail and his nesting dolls.

In the tug of memory a man on the street pulls his sleeve. Hey Canada, voulez-vous changez des argent? Thumb tight across the bills in his hand. Canada remembers the college student who traded Canadian money for defunct lottery tickets. The hockey fan takes two steps backwards. "Merci," he says and tucks the receipt into his breast pocket. She turns away, the steam disappears, her hair is dry.

The hockey fan walks across the lobby. The elevator takes off quietly, slowly lifts him, up, up to the long corridor which overlooks the hotel garden, creeping delivery trucks, sparkling snow. The hockey fan strides the corridor to his room at the tip of the H, where the Grail, his Grail, waits for him. Wednesday the hockey game, Thursday the ballet. On Friday the circus, Saturday back to Helsinki. But now he is in Leningrad, city of intentions, book in hand, doll in his pocket, walking down the corridors of the Hotel Pulkovskaya to the room where the Grail waits for him. Wrapped with plain brown paper and tucked carefully into the corner of his suitcase, the Grail waits for him to open his bag, shed the paper, release her wink and twinkle to the misty air.

The Hockey Fan Hears the Muse

An answer is plain as the nose snuffling thick in his head. The radio broadcasts, the Hot Stove League, the two-minute interview, the post-game wrap-up, the leisurely between-period profile, dogs and all – or horses, sometimes there are horses – the yelling and hollering in rinks, in dressing rooms, in school playgrounds, the arguments in front of the common room, the family room, the beer parlour, television. The fan eats, sleeps and dreams stories. Consumes stories, gobbles them up, can't get enough. Reading lips on television you know inside stories, you know what the coach really said. Or in the pools you can play owner, pick your own team, curse and yatter at your bad picks, at players who don't perform, at the ungodly run of injuries.

Given to tell stories, he imagines a future and weaves into the present remembered and invented flashes of the past. In these stories he becomes part of a team again: reader and writer, playing.

Yes, in these stories you, dear reader, play at your own pace, hear the soft sounds of a tale unfolding, listen to the stroke of letters grazing the icy page. You make it go, make it go.

I see, she sings, I see you pass me, she sings, I see you past me. You pass me this book, she sings, skate on by, pass me the puck, pass me, pace me, she sings, paste me, taste me, how you gonna take me.

Hockey Is a Transition Game

Stories are hand-me-down gifts you wear that don't wear out. His father used to tell stories about how poor they were in the old days. "So poor," he said, "we were so poor we didn't have hockey sticks. Used bent willow branches and horse apples for a puck and snot string for laces. We were so poor we ate turnips all the time. At Christmas we got cranberry sauce with our turnips and Mother cut off the bottoms of our pockets so we'd have something to play with."

His father grew up on the parklands of northern Saskatchewan. There he met a woman, not far from Prince Albert, edging on the bush they were to move into, where the hockey fan was born, farther north, bum shining. In the winter he travelled by bum shining. You hook onto the back bumper of a car or bus, and squat down, ride on your boots, glide over the snow through the fingering cold to tennis ball street hockey with Carnation milk tins marking the goal, make a big save with a beat-up baseball glove, wait for the chance to be a rink rat and boom the puck off the boards, drive a slap shot from blue line to the short side.

Now things have changed. Kids travel everywhere and they don't bum shine outside. They ride inside buses, trains and shiny planes. They don't go to the pond, they go across the pond. The invitation comes. The hockey fan is determined. He pulls his hands out of his pockets and packs his bags.

The Lineup

For tonight's game we have three generations: the personal pronouns, the shadows and shades of the self, shifty shape-shifter, and you. Not dressed, for the moment, are thee and thou, but they linger, naked, in the tones of voice. "I" is the hockey fan. In his home uniform he is father to Mark and Denis, sons number 1 and 2, and to Shannon and Andrea, daughters 1 and 2. He, "I," is fond of twosomes and doubles and thinks his family is number one. Some would say he could be anyone. Others think he's a nobody, a non-entity, certainly nothing to look at, but you can decide for yourself, you paid the admission. In this arena the customer's always right.

One of the doubles I is fond of hangs on the peg in his dressing room. A hockey sweater his mother kept for him, yellow with frayed cuffs. A green cloverleaf on the chest says Mintos 1950–51, Champs. I is fond of this sweater because it was his first and because Denis plays for a team in green and yellow, the Prince Albert Raiders. (Denis wears a mask with green and yellow stripes, a stainless steel cage, moulded fibreglass chin. His mask echoes the gear of a mediaeval warrior: the ceremonial helmet on the Sutton Hoo burial ship, blank eyes staring at us from the sixth century. The mask: a double doubling.) In 1950–51, history says a team called the Mintos played out of Prince Albert. But since fiction frowns on such coincidences, I wants you to overlook them. The other sweater on that hook is grey, an image of Beethoven with hair flying as he skates along, a gift from Lorraine before they were married. I loves that one too.

I could go on and tell you that his parents were married not far from Prince Albert so we stretch things across three generations and make two doubles, mother and father and sons and daughters on one hand, and father and mother and daughters and sons on the other, say, like the runners on some skates or the two teams out there now. They circle and whirl, pass and shoot, stop and start. The fans divide themselves and speak at once, pro and con. Against that mix of voices – you hear them in the background – the narrator tells I through the special headset announcers wear to get on with the action. So I goes on. You come too.

Tonight's game is mostly on the road, riding, I says, but one is always involved in home games on the road. The food is often bad so one wishes one were there or someplace else. You of course sit at home, warm by the fireplace, sip your tea or scotch – I recommends Johnny Walker Black or Glenfiddich – while we skate on the thin page of ice. You join us, he and she and I and you. So we feast together. Sing together. Lick the icing on the cake. Spring thee and thou from the locker, together.

Over the Polar Seas

JANUARY 13 1985   Over the Pole and the glories of the winter sun footlight the clouds. We slide on that golden glow and race the day to Seattle. I sip scotch and soda. My surprise yesterday at the brightness of the Helsinki airport. I rushed to drink fresh water, the cold drops sharp on my lips. The previous four days in Russia I drank only tea and whiskey, cognac and tea, spit and spit when I brushed my teeth. Now I draw the scotch slowly over my tongue, form liquid vowels while fragments of the old world circle and whirl, images as fresh and golden as the clouds outside my window. This floating brightness recalls our hotel in Leningrad, the Pulkovskaya, the newest of all the hotels on our tour. It was built by Finns and designed to please the taste of Westerners: a bathroom which shines and sparkles, a Monet reproduction on the wall – sailboats, leaves on the trees, the colours of spring. Outside the plane now the sun and clouds make a winter gold, crisp and laced with fine streaks of crimson and rose. The colours of dawn stretch across the sky.

We carry the day with us westward and land in Seattle, mid-afternoon, down ramps and stairs, escalators and runways, down to the luggage carousel and the waiting lines. Customed and stamped and luggaged we take up, again, our version of the North American story: we bus the green hills from Seattle north to Vancouver and then fly east to Edmonton. The food and drinks, strange in their familiarity, taste fine.

We assume again the old story: travellers from Europe, we make our way into the heart of the continent, though this time we have reversed the old pattern – turn the Atlantic story back on itself and go west to east, inland from the Pacific. And then in another turn of the story, we drive south from Edmonton to Red Deer. We ride in my T-Bird south to begin the new year with a fresh vision, new version of the old continental trek. In the New World garden we fly in my T-Bird, drive and dream of the gardens and arenas, the Grail tucked tight in my bag.

The end of the journal: the beginning of the book.

The Hockey Fan Reflects on Beginnings

It all begins with guts. The looping scrawl of prairie rivers tucked inside the cavity of your belly, chewing your food, as they say munch, munch. Just chomping and chewing and squirting and squeezing and squooshing mush diddle diddle mush, moving a lung, tickling the blood stream blood red, trickling along the vine of veins. Squish dee doodle go the guts. Squoik. Down the hatch, down the tube, the same old story: the teacher smears the ping pong ball with glycerine and squeezes it into the inner tube, bicycle tube, red with some blue blotches, tries to squeeze it down the tube, muscles working, grimace, grunt, stuck in the old tube, slammed shut, bunged up. Guts belong in your belly and you want to leave them there where they belong. Don't spill them however much you long to tell it all.

In Flin Flon he begins another beginning, a legendary place where the garden is called, yes, the Main Arena and the streets are paved with hockey pucks and gold. Or so the story goes and you never get away from the stories. Right now, on the desk in front of me, a May 1989 article in *The Hockey News* tells how the Swift Current Broncos come from the smallest town to win the Memorial Cup since the Flin Flon Bombers won in 1957. You see? You see?

> *Flin Flon? they say.*
>
> *Why the only people I know from Flin Flon are hockey players and hookers.*
>
> *My mother is from Flin Flon, you say.*
>
> *Long pause.*
>
> *And what position does she play?*
>
> *Left Wing, Right Wing, Defence, Goal: the goal of life is.*

Of course you expect stories from people raised in a town

named after the nickname of a fictional hero. The hockey fan began in place and a good beginning it was. His mother worked hard to bear him. She carried him warm in her belly and then he was bare and she lugged him home in her arms. Her travail gave him from her to you, sitting there, lying there. A good beginning it was, but sometimes she can barely stand him.

A Point about Style

The announcer begins in the third person and then shifts into second: "The Oilers are piling in front of the net to set up a screen or make a deflection and you have to be tough in there. Why not talk a little to the goalie and try to throw him off his game, maybe cause a breakdown in concentration?"

You are the second person, of course, and I am the first, and those guys over there are third, but when you stand here beside me and we point to those guys we can sight along the same finger and see sort of the same thing, so why stick you in the middle of our sights, still within spearing range? That's how people get hurt.

Replay

You drag into bed with your duffle bag for a pillow and lie awake for hours waiting for mother/father/brother/sister to say you can get up now, and you do, you throw off the hockey stick and leap out of bed, jump at the smell of sizzling bacon, the flap of pancakes or the snap of crackle and pop. You strip off skates, goalie pads, hockey pants, jockstrap, woolen sweater: all before your morning pee.

You pull on jockstrap, shin pads, Eaton's/Simpson-Sears catalogues. Strap them on snug with sealer rings, elastic bands, old suspenders, a girdle cut into strips. Tug the sweater over your head, number 9: you are Rocket Richard, Gordie Howe, Teeder Kennedy, Johnny Bucyk, Andy Bathgate, Jean Ratelle, Bobby Hull.

Out the door, the hinge squawks and you walk four eight twelve seventeen miles to the rink through drifts piled three five seven eleven feet high with the temperature thirty fifty sixty below zero Fahrenheit, little brother/sister carrying your skates and you clean the ice when you get there, shovel it off with willow branches, homemade scrapers, a Massey Harris tractor and front-end loader, a tablespoon, a shovel, a spade, a scraper. You sweep it swishing with hockey sticks, push brooms, corn brooms, curling brooms, tree branches, cardboard boxes. You line up behind a slab of plywood and heave.

Or a trip to the rink is Mother arguing with your ten-year-old cold. Bristling you carry your skates and stick curved with a sharp edge, a toothpick, the skinny one-piece slapped together with friction tape. You walk quicker than cough, skate quicker than a runny nose.

Haul the old tire, the Model T/Fargo truck/International tractor tire down to the edge of the river/dugout/canal/slough/creek/lake/pond. Take strands of dried grass sticking through the snow and sheets torn from little brother's shin pads, and more sheets, hold still and start a blaze in the tire, stoke it up. Gaze through tears into the fire, fold back the tongue of your skates as far as they go, gag and cough. You wiggle your toes to keep them warm, wiggle again to shiver them snug into the stiff boot of your brother/sister/cousin/neighbour's hand-me-down skates.

They arrive in clumps of two and three. For goal posts: Carnation milk tins, or Borden's Elsie moo cow mooing, piles of snow, blocks of firewood, your little brother's boots. For a puck: horse apples, a small cow pattie, a tennis ball, a piece of coal, little brother's mitten, a hunk of slag, a tin can. The tire blazes away, you press right into the black smoke to thaw the ice from your fly. Your piss freezes midstream and you snap it off, a sword to skewer enemies, a popsicle for false friends or little brother.

Skates sing like fingernails clawing a chalkboard, like a slow train on rusty tracks. Your stick breaks the first time you touch the puck. The puck breaks in half the first time it hits the goal post. A train chuffing belch and chug snores by you and you skewer the smoke, stretch it over the skating rink with large sweeping curves. The smoke roof keeps snow off for more than two months, the rink so hot now, you say, you have to play in your underwear/jockstrap/girdle/brassiere or stark naked, skinny slipping on the pond/lake/river/weir/tarn/creek/canal/dugout/slough. Inside you try to find the elusive rise of Tina's breast. You fumble leather mitts and woolen liners hockey-glove clumsy over the front of her new parka. Her many-coloured scarf and her turtleneck sweater tickle your chin. Her nose dribbles when she nuzzles your cheek tinglecold and warm at the same time, and you like it the way you like a bodycheck. Wakes you up, surprises you into/out of yourself.

Or you go to the shack where Mr. Shomperlen sloshes around in his huge boots – always buy the biggest size, he says, you get more for your money – and stokes the fire in the barrel stove. It whistles and pings when you throw snow from your skates, ticks and ticks into a steaming hush. Mr. Shomperlen loves his work. He heats the shack cozy warm and pampers the ice. He slushes over cracks and holes with his trowel, makes the ice creamy smooth, baby bum smooth. Inside you try to get through parka and ski pants to Tina's bum wiggle, her wet wiggle nose, but someone comes in. The door squeaks open in a draft of stumping skates, clump, clump on wood. Someone always clumps in checking and you wiggle away just that far and the fire leaves you warm and wiggling and wishing.

Outside, the game swirls in fluffy snow and turns with dozens of players, each team a motley collection of flapping scarves, ski pants, breeks, cowboy boots, rubber overshoes, the metal hooks scrick, scrick, scricking, fur-lined hoods, woolen and leather mittens, wool pants so heavy the kids' eyes droop: a cast of dozens, a catalogue of catalogues and sealer rings. The score rises, a wrangled swap of players back and forth and skating, running scrickety all the time, the score getting higher, and rules shout down the wind.

No raising, no slashing, keep your stick down.

No bodychecks, no roughing up little kids except brothers/sisters/brats/pests/nuisances/crybabies.

No lying down in goal, one person in goal or none at all. No fair playing goal with boots on.

No face-off, go back to your end after a goal, give us a chance to wind up.

Shoot the puck over the boards you have to find it or send your little brother/sister. Sisters and brothers get to ask Mrs. Forster for water or the time, is it supper time.

Pass it, Puck Hog.

No tripping, slashing, high-sticking, boarding, crosschecking.

Stop only for nosebleeds, lost pucks.

Into the thirties, the score runs into the forties. You join the game from night to night, revised at recess on the rocks, on the way home at noon hour, in the can. The great plays undergo sea changes and reversals, run again over and over time for visions and revisions: the cocoa, the fat lips, the broken sticks, skate laces knotted and knotted, bumps and thumps, fingers and ears bite so hard you swear they have teeth, dentist drills crack through your head from both sides, nails hammered into fingers and thumbs, and hungry?

Yes, bellyroaring for food, you wipe your blades with an old gunny sack, a piece of cardboard, little brother's toque, his scarf. You walk home on stumps, thump and squeak, thumpety thump like Frosty the Snowman through the thirty forty seventy below temperature and seven eight fourteen foot drifts. Your fingers tingle at changes in temperature and humidity. You hustle to the warm kitchen table for hot chocolate and peanut butter sandwiches and sit around the stove, stuff yourself full with fat warm stories. The smell of bread baking filters through little brother's blubbering, the reek of burnt tires, toebite and fingerbite, cocoa and jam. You breathe deep in the warmth of the hot, hot stove.

First Blood, 1950

Unused to the new zippered style, the hockey fan catches himself up, short, draws blood, seeks help howling from his giggling sister. Two hands are not enough. He maketh a storm, he prayeth devoutly for buttons, he contemplateth religious conversion.

The street is his first rink, and later he skates with brothers and sisters on the ice of the lake. A fire burns black and sweet inside an old tire. This is the hot tire league. He gathers sticks from the bush beside the tracks, clumps of dead grass from the shoreline.

The lake isn't theirs but the rink is. It parks right beside their garden (a potato garden mainly, big flat rock in the middle, some turnips and cabbages) and they have more kids than the other families, a fruitful bunch – Merle and Gwen and Carol and Wayne and him, the brat they say, and Allen at home with Mom waiting his turn and waiting for Cheryl, the baby of them all – so the rink is theirs twice over. On that rink they skate and skate, and stump home through clenched teeth for Dad to rub their piggies warm, rub them with snow to warm them, his soft black eyes warm through the tears. And the next day they go over the banked rocks and through wind and snow to skate again on the lake, their blades rasp, rasping on the ice.

On that lake there are always other rinks – one under the trestle, two or three down at Mile 84, at least two near the Island and God knows how many on the Ross Lake side. And that's only one lake. Uptown there's Hapnot Lake, Schist Lake at Channing, Flin Flon Lake in Creighton. The rink near the Creek Bridge in Lakeside. Ponds and sloughs and ditches and gravel pits. Lots of rinks and plenty of winter.

One year the lake freezes over with no snow cover. The boundaries gone he chases the puck for miles, wind in his chest, the ice slick as glass, crystal clicking, blade cutting. On the rhythmic singing of the ice the puck slides and slides and slides. On that singing lake in the bristle of wind you can push and stride, in the streaming cold, you can stretch out and skate and you do.

The Bombardier and Other Stories

The call comes and he is picked but the name is a problem to ten-year-old ears. He knows there are men called bomber dears who ride in airplanes and drop bombs. They are dears, he has heard them called dears.

But this is a thing, not a person. Perhaps this thing is a strange animal, like a reindeer for hauling hockey players. The Bombers are the big team in town: he will travel on the Bomber Deer, a beast more powerful than red snout Rudolph or any of the Christmas livestock. Or maybe this thing is a new-fangled machine from John Deere tractors – a quick new Deere for hockey players? A Bomber Deere?

He sees it isn't a tractor or a person or an animal. Blunt nose snouting out over skis, drive wheels with wide rubber tracks. A tank without a gun. Not cute like Bambi or sexy like his blinky-eyed mother. More like a draft horse, a Volkswagen beetle blown up into a fat balloon. A Bomba Deer. Travels on the winter road: Flin Flon north and west to Island Falls, back again, over the lakes and portages – we say *pórt•age* – seventy-five drafty miles each way.

His team plays on Saturday night and then again on Sunday morning and wins both games. Like the Bombers, they always win. After the Sunday game they tour the dam: huge generators spinning, the charging Churchill River. Two enormous sturgeon butt against the glass. The river tumbles January steam and the lines power over lakes and snow all the way home: a little piggy stretched over the wires to market and home again to the town where the lights burn night and day.

On the road home they sweep across lakes and crank around corners on the portages. Bounced and jostled, one kid gets sick. They jump out for fresh air – pictures in *The Northern Lights* show how a Linn tractor crashes through the ice, but they clamber out and the lake stands solid as the earth.

Later, at home under the corner street lamp, he reads the match book cover which says the lights burn night and day in this strange town, the town where he lives. He reads the cover, a little light house says Eddy Match Company. It is five o'clock, the street lights are on. The match book says the town gets power from Island Falls on the Churchill River. But it says nothing about the hockey games or the sturgeon in the tank or the boys scrambling onto the sweeping ice of the lake or the crash of water through the dam and the quiet mist floating upward, and no word at all about the bouncing blue Bomba Deer.

Down the bank on foot along the CNR tracks and over the trestle and then across the lake to the Ross Lake Curling Club to get warm, and then up the hill and into Poirier's to get warm, and the long trek up 3rd Avenue Hill, fetch a pail of water and up again, the 100 Steps, and down across Main Street, past the General Hospital and St. Mary's to the Main Arena, hockey bag dangling on the edge of his CCM stick.

walking
dum de doo be dummmm

They bounce around the back of the delivery van, a big box with no windows, bouncing. Today they are entrepreneurs. Early this morning they set out in the minus 40 chill to cut Christmas trees, the square-tired car thumping along in the morning frost: they set out to raise money for a road trip. (Nick sells a tree, sticks it in a snowbank in the backyard. At night he goes back, borrows the tree and sells it to someone else a few streets over. Three times, you triple your money.) But before noon a spruce tree rejected the caress of Nick's axe, threw it back at him and sliced open his knee. They sent him to hospital stretched out stiff in the back seat of the thumping car. And now the rest of the team rides home in the truck, they bounce and ricochet, search for balance, smash the Christmas trees. Dream of road games, a hot stove.

dum dum
dum dum

The Hockey Fan on Site

1 When Canada won the gold medal in the World Junior Championships, Helsinki 1985, I was there. You've seen the TV clip that shows a group of fans waving the Canadian flag. Mark waves one end, Ed the fireman waves the other. Denis is perched just behind the flag wavers. You can't see me because I'm higher up and off to your left, waving to the camera, just out of your line of vision. The game wasn't over then, at that moment, though the clock was winding down. At that moment, Terry Simpson was coaching, behind the bench. Now in January 1990, five years later, he coaches Denis in Prince Albert. They're on a West Coast road swing: tonight in Victoria, Wednesday in Seattle, on to Portland, Kennewick, Spokane. That's where they are in 1990. For his part, Mark follows his camera around Calgary, and me, I am here with you.

Still photographs and filmic images, like pronouns and people, are shifty things. Both kinds move you and filmic images move themselves at the same time, so you think you see what's happening in Helsinki, the game live from the arena. Mark's photograph freezes a car accident on the front page of the newspaper. By a sleight of eye you see from his angle of vision but you don't see him. The photographer as invisible man. Of course you know you're not there in either case, even as you watch the curl of the maple leaf on that flag, or see the paramedics reach out to the child in the car.

Put it another way. "We take you live to the Gardens," the announcer says and the screen shows the play from one camera angle, and then a second camera takes the 180 degrees not in the first shot. You see how the attacking player's quick deke to the left throws the defender off balance, you follow the wrist shot high to the stick side. Then you see the defenceman hooked, his ankle slapped by the winger breaking in from the blue line. Click back and forth, sew them together and there it is, a small story sutured up snug and tight.

But the camera always keeps secrets, turns a blind eye to hack and slash, the glove in the mush, the jab to the calf. Lifts a deaf ear to taunts and threats. And sneaky – you never see the one you're looking through. Can't smell a thing. Cameras are just like referees, you wonder what game they're watching. Who runs those cameras anyway? Who hits the switch to make the suture? Who referees the switcher? Who switches referees?

You have to park at the arena and pay for the seat to think you're getting the whole deal.

2 Photographic images still and moving fracture the universe, cut it into bits and pieces. That film clip from Helsinki compresses space and gives the illusion of present action. It also sketches the future. Next year the World Championship will be in Saskatchewan cities: Prince Albert, Saskatoon, Regina, Swift Current, Moose Jaw. You will see the world's teams there. I think of our road games to Dauphin or Brandon, three hundred or four hundred miles distant, our axes whack and crash through the Christmas trees, we heave and dodge around the back of the truck. The bone-numbing cold. But next year the Worlds are in Saskatchewan, the junior hockey world jammed into one province. Czechs, Finns, Swedes, Yankees, Russians, Canucks. Next year, I see it now, the cameras will catch the curve of the arena in Saskatoon, the wide open spaces of the bald-headed prairies. They will show ribboned roads in the moonlight, asphalt swirling with dandruffy snow, ghost shapes on a purple moor.

Those images will leave out the dance of the northern lights, the crack and growl of ice on the lake or river, shenanigans in the shack, the strike of striding steel. Here is hockey, they will say, and give you indoor shots. But don't be fooled. Hockey won't be caught in an image, frozen and fixed or thawed and quick. Take, for example, that Helsinki clip. You are at one end of the camera – I'm waving at you and you don't even give me a glance. You treat me as if I'm not there, or here. As if I were in the photo of the lake, a swimmer at the bottom.

But I am here still, and others are here too, and if you listen carefully to the grain of the voice squeezed in between letters, the crack of consonants and roll of vowels, the pauses and intakes of breath, in this very place you will hear, say, my mother/my father telling a story – together they smile at you. Yes, if you listen you can join us right here, set us moving, reading and riding, wreathing and writhing.

Home Games

We pile into the Studebaker, tug coats around ourselves, pinch legs and bottoms together, listen to hear if the motor will start. It catches, roars, the heater whines.

"All right you guys, stop breathing," Wayne says. He scratches at the windshield, peels thin slivers of snow just above the heater vents. The snow forms as fast as he scrapes it off.

He eases the car into gear, we move slowly *ka-thump ka-thump* and he slumps to peer through the half-arc of clear windshield and *ka-thumpety* throws open the door to signal a left turn *ka-thumpety* we *ka-thumpety* down the hill, scrunched into collars, pinched bums, cold noses, crossed arms, fists *ka-thumpety* breathing *ka-thumpety ka-thumpety*.

The Rat Room

We live in the Rat Room when we aren't poking pool or playing hockey. It's a secret place: after the games and during public skating it's our room and we keep everyone else out. Two light bulbs, an open piss-trough with a wooden step in front, benches nailed to the wall, a few coat hooks, some bent nails, and thick black conveyor belt laid on the floor – we have it all to ourselves. The Rat Room is the home place.

After we clean the ice, it too is ours but Merle steals the puck again and again with sweep checks takes it away. Finally we give up our straight-ahead-puck-hog-deke-and-shift, see the stretch of ice and throw passes to our mates. Brothers slip the puck away so quick.

———

The rink rat gets elected secretary-treasurer (he drives a typewriter) and types out the tickets for the hockey pool: Bombers 1–0, 2–0, 3–0 and all the combinations, winning and losing, up to 10. He pounds the hell out of the period key to make a page of little squares, and on each of these squares types a score. Each of them a possible story, one hundred little stories neatly coded, Est. for Estevan, P..A. for Prince Albert, Sask. for Saskatoon, Mel. for the Millionaires, Reg. for the Queen City. And then the numbers: each story enclosed by the periods, as you would expect. Folds each story. Then sticks each one into a small envelope, the size dentists put yanked-out teeth into. Then he shuffles and divides them into piles of ten. Each rink rat sells his tickets, two bits a shot, writes the buyer's name on the envelope. So the guy who has the final score, say Bombers 5 Saskatoon 3, wins ten bucks. And the rink rats hoard the rest to buy rink rat jackets. Blue and white, raglan sleeves, with a rat smiling red and white on the chest. A neat crest made of chenille.

Each home game adds to the treasury, the old jewel box swiped from his sister, a little brass key. The Bombers win most of their games, some by big scores. They ding eleven, say, or twelve, and the rats pocket all the cash. In high scoring games they cheer like hell for more goals. Hey, people say after the game, who won the pool? Some guy on Hapnot Street, say the rats, works in the smelter or the zinc plant, something like that.

On the ides of each month the rats cut the ice and shave off the hills and lumps that build up, the glop along the boards. The ice-cutting machine, a big steel affair, huddles and grumbles, blades rotating under its belly. Murray and Milt push it forward, razoring around the rink. Rink rats gather up the snow and push, heave and drag it to the box, shovel it in. Leon and Bob dance with steel scrapers, slide and turn and glide while the electrician tries to fix the cutter. You learn to be careful with those scrapers. Give yourself a good whack in the shins, a slam in the knackers, you're not careful.

Hipcheck

You can tell the mood she is in by the way she racks the balls. Slam, snap and click as she centres on the six spot is our cue not to slam shots off the table, not to stuff the cue ball in Tom's coat pocket and especially not to swear. You can tease Missus, make her hooded eyes crackle, thin lips crinkle into smile, and she in turn will bank you off a wall with a soft hipcheck or give you a hug, all five feet of her, or just as you line up a three-to-the-side, pinch your bum if the angle is right. Missus is a poet, her touch so light she can spot the six ball and hold the triangle tight – her presence is felt.

But swearing calls for sterner measures and springs her into new rhythms: firing snooker balls in all directions, whacking gawky boys across the back she gives us the word and the word is Missus – "O nooo, you no swear in my poolroom, bugger off this place leetle bastar."

And the room becomes quiet and her mouth droops a little at the corners and she stands behind the glass counter putting chocolate bars into line and slowly the clicking begins again, soft clicks now, straight bank shots cut fine into the corner, Johnny Cash crooning softly under the pin ball jangle and bong, games finish and begin, and again Missus, our mistress, steady at the head of the table, cheeks soft and passive, plump hands patting the balls gently on the felt and rolling the triangle forward, offers us peace, her eyes smiling blue – "Thas nice boys, doan fight, feenish now, thas nice, put up cue."

By Bus

He and Bob room together on a trip to Dauphin but they lose so later they drink beer with guys from the other team who don't have girl friends. Crash in a hotel two in a bed and he pukes hanging over into the garbage can and Bob scrambles to the other end for fresh air – sleeps with feet in his face, head to toe for fresh air.

All the way home, the bus slips over the road and grinds through towns, gears down for Ashville/Ethelbert/Pine River/ Cowan/Renwer/Minitonas/Swan River/Bowsman/Birch River/ Mafeking, stops at the Overflowing River, frozen solid, and then drives through the Bog, the bitter, bitter Bog, The Pas/Wanless/ Cranberry Portage/Bakers Narrows, the road frozen and the bus slides and jiggles and bounces around, slams into snow drifts like waves on a lake *a whump a whump*. The bus too warm and the road trip home is a long road home, riding, riding over the driven snow, writing scribble dribble diddle on the snowdrift plain, the hockey fan came riding, riding, riding through the sweet puck night, the moon a sliver of gold.

Calgary to Helsinki

DECEMBER 26 1984 In the darkness before dawn, 4:00 AM and minus 24, we pack the van with hockey equipment and head out for the Calgary airport. We're on our way to the old world and our first move is to pack up the luggage. Then in the morning darkness we board an Air Canada flight east into day and dusk. I leave a trace of letters: from Calgary International in the morning, later in the mid-afternoon gloom from Mirabel. We handle luggage at every turn. Boxing Day becomes The Day of Bags.

The luggage, the luggage: the verbs inside the noun. We gauge time by the lifting of bags. We have eighty pieces in all for a group of 50 people: hockey bags and hockey sticks, medical supplies for the team, and suitcases and duffle bags – all decorated with little pink woolen ribbons. We load and unload. The ribbons flap and twist their pink hair as we heave bags off and on carousels, buses, trucks.

We arrive in Helsinki, 11:25 AM local time, December 27. Bus to Tampere. This landscape looks like the Canadian shield, with scattered houses added, as if the shield were being farmed. Rocky outcrops, spruce and pine. The scene that runs past the bus window, as Earle Birney might say, is "clean and cosy as a Christmas card."

On the city outskirts, a big sign, "Postipankki." The driver loses his way, but after loops and curls and hills we arrive, 30 minutes late, at a small motor hotel near two hockey arenas. Icehalls they are called in Finnish. The name echoes with meadhalls, spears and slashing, bragging and tall tales, the slaying of dragons – a place where a bunch of drunken hackers get together to drink beer and tell lies. The beer, knocked back and gargled, unlocks the wordhoards: the glory of the Gar-Denes, Spear Danes, stories of the spear.

Other guys get the fun. You've got responsibilities. Keep them out of the slot, out of the crease. That's what you're there for. Keep it clean in front.

>*Other guys fool around, tool around*
>*Even dipsydoo'le around*
>*I got the stay put*
>*Lowdown leadfoot*
>*Stay-at-home defenceman*
>*Won't let me play around*
>*The lowdown deadfoot*
>*Stay-at-home defenceman*
>*Blooooooooooze.*

———————————

   And then one fall the CNR Dayliner, a speedy passenger train takes him to The Pas, and the old milk train to yellow rooms in the Winnipeg YMCA, cheap restaurants, the Winnipeg Braves, the St. Boniface Canadiens exhibiting themselves in Flin Flon, the United College Redmen, and then west and south by bus now to the Boissevain Border Kings, and later, west again to play left wing for a literary magazine in Regina (the magazine is *The Sphinx,* the people Sphinxters, the hockey team the Obfuskaters), then back to Winnipeg where he breaks retirement to play for the graduate students against the English profs the year before Al Purdy is there to write a poem about the game, and west again, bang up against the cowboy Rockies to Red Deer and the Big Belly No Hit League, the NHL at last.

   As a parent he travels again, over the Rocks into B.C., across Alberta, Saskatchewan, Manitoba, to Ontario, to Europe. By telephone to Quebec and British Columbia, Washington and Oregon, Germany and Czechoslovakia. Always on the road, ride, riding.

The Mintos, the little yellow sweater with a cloverleaf, Champs 1950–51. The Kinsmen, blue and gold. The Doghouse, yes, blue with red and white, sponsored by the local teenage hotdog and hamburger hangout, fries with gravy, Flin Flon Juvenile Champs, 1959–60. The Rink Rats. The Flin Flon Midget Bombers, Manitoba Midget A Champs, 1959–60, maroon and white. The Winnipeg Braves, black and orange. The St. Boniface Canadiens, a Christmas exhibition game against Flin Flon, in borrowed skates, le bleu blanc rouge. The United College Redmen, University of Manitoba Inter-Faculty Champs, 1963–64, red and white. The Boissevain Border Kings, gold and black. The Obfuskaters, a motley crew. I bought my first curved hockey stick. Mark and I played on the outdoor rink, he got away on me, walked on the snowy crusts across the park. The Red Deer College Big Bellies, gold with black, stretched.

What the Coach Said

1   I'm the coach you men, your mentor, and I mean you guys
well, I want ya to win lots of gold and I can do it without bein'
mean. Seldom have my boys heard a discouraging word but I
undress you when you need it, I dress you down so the deer and
the antelope play. Doan like roman buffaloes tho and that goes for
you too Sproxton whatever kinda name that is. Lace them up now,
snug as a girdle on a horse's bum. Left, right, left, right. Get ready
now. You make a whole row of x's on each skate, snug them up
tight. The laces crisscross your crotch and make a fly, you tie the
lace in a bow at the top. Let the string hang down, swing down,
low down, derry, derry down. Okay, no roman around like a herd
of buffaloes out there gettin dozy. You gotta pay attenshun to the
line, stop 'em at the line. I want the forwards coming back and the
dee moving up, five man units, skate 'em in the corners. I want
forechecking – that means two guys in, I tole you before, first man
on the man, second guy on the puck, third man high, stop waven
you goofball and lissen up. There's gold in them checks. Muck in
the corners and weel clean up on these muckie mucks and the fat
cat owners. Forwards come back, dee keep yr arses outa the
goalie's face. Make sure you cover the slot, doan want no sunburnt
goalies this team. Warm up now and remember Arnason hit the
net, ain't hunting ducks, give Redlite a chance to grabba few.

2   You

You guys

You guys r

You guys r so

You guys r so lazy

I betcha shit the bed and push it out with your feet.

I betcha my grandmother could beat you to the puck.

I betcha my dead grandmother could beat ya to the puck and knock ya on yr ass.

You guys r so lazy wer gonna go for a leetle run later, gonna chase ya with the bus, gonna hike ya down the road, gonna wake you up.

You guys been gettin' away with suckin' around so far, but yr gonna get burnt you don't lay on the body.

Wimps, pussies, the whole lot of you, standin' aroun', fingers up yr bums.

Lace those guys in the slot.

Nail 'em at the line.

Bang 'em in the corners.

Show some life out there.

You bin playin' with it all night again?

Gonna send you guys to bed with boxin' gloves on.

Fred what're you thinkin' about? Yr heart in it? You hear music or somethin', dancin' around like a guy doin' the watusi. Watch yrself eh.

Cooley's bin workin' hard, puttin' the body into it, you guys do some soul searchin' too.

Hay I tole and I tole you, cards after the game. Put those suckers down. Nasty habit you got, canasta brain. Big lug. Runnin' around out there like a bear cub with his first hard on.

3   This is the third and time we did somethin'. I'm gonna shorten the bench and shorten the lives of some of you characters. Shorten your dinks by an inch have a hole in your bellies. Watcha doing. Fall asleep at the throttle? Asleep at the crotch more like it, you guys are so lazy the pussies have to lick you to wake you up. Shit the bed every day. Some of you guys. Asshole. White Dwarf. Black Hole. Crow bait. Ding bat. Bonehead. Doorknob. Right Angle. Parallelogram. Rhomboid. Ramboid. Bird Brain. Yr head's like a crow's nest. Dingle Balls. Straw on the outside and shit on the inside. Cosine. Punch Card. Bubble Sort. Vacuum Tube. Cement Head.

Blood and Guts

The hockey fan likes blood and guts, especially the enemy's guts and blood. But you can't always tell who the enemy is. One time I got highsticked in the chops and fell to the ice in a heap. Our trainer came running out and when he saw I wasn't bleeding, he gave me a little shot in the nose, trying to draw some blood so the other guy would get five minutes.

Once I crashed into the boards with another guy and we started slugging at each other. A woman behind the screen said, "Beat the snot outa that creep," and I could tell she liked my style. I guess we would have killed each other, but the referee got in the way – stuck his finger in my eye and his thumb up my nose, which wasn't too bad considering it was supposed to be a fight, except that he was the brother-in-law of the guy that I was trying to kill and was trying to kill me.

H/o/c/k/e/y/ F/a/n/

hoke   short for hokum

choke   a no-no

chek   chek, chek, chek, the only way to win

kych   but still interesting

hock   spittooooeee

koch ye   says the referee, koch ye red handed, ya bad bandit

kech   with yr big trapper, kech the speedy winger from behind

chyk   a puck bunny

chok   full of good things

chyk chek   what a bunny costs

hoe   the way some guys handle their sticks – hack, chop, slash.
What Beowulf says, his grim sword dripping blood

hyck   up, yr pants, or what happens in your throat ya don't chek
yrself

hycky   what sucking gives ya

hoy   tea toitea

heck   what you get when ya tie a game

nack   what some guys got and some don't

noy   what the other fans does to ya

foe   what the other fans is

okay   the trainer asks after he slugs ya in the snout, okay? okay?

hack   get the point, a tired writer, a goonish writer

fen   a convention of hack writers, a marsh, a swamp

kan   what ya falls on when hacked. Another name for athletic supporter, fan. The room with flooded bowls and wall-to-wall poems, where people reads and writes

han   what ya gets when ya makes a big save or scores a goal, a big han

nock   on my door anytime

cane   what a goon raises, sugar

ken   i don't know, i don't have a clue, is beyond me

neck   pains me to say it

feck   less than an idiot

foke   what goes to the game

fey   the guy with quick feet and soft hands

yen   what ya gets for beers after a game

yak   what ya says to the refs and the other team

fack   what yr manager tells ya at contract time, the fack is

kaf   a small boy cow, what takes yr place after ya get the facks

chyn   where ya gets it when ya sticks yr nose in

ake   what happens when you gets dinged if ya don't wear a kan

cake   how ya walks when ya blow the other team out, what ya can't have and eat too

fake   hokey

hokey yoke eh?

A Stitch in Time

1 The scars tell the story. Nicks and cuts scratched into flesh, worms buried and burrowing under the hide. My hide is an open book. The first chapter starts on my chin, one and one-quarter inches long, one inch below the lower lip, tilting downward a little to the left, from a butt end in the deep slot. Fourteen stitches I snipped off one week later in Winnipeg, 1957. "You should get that looked to right away," said Red, hands on my face. "It's a deep cut. You need stitches, you'll have to shave around it when you get older if you don't get it stitched up right away."

2 And the one you don't see, the secret chapter, runic, hidden behind the right ear. Delivered by skate, the Main Arena, Flin Flon. A red letter day. Some guys don't skate very well. If you lift your heels you lose speed. Somehow his skate met my head. At the company hospital they put a plug in. You can feel it with your fingers. Run your fingers through my hair.

3 Sutures are called catgut, a tough cord made from sheep's intestines. Sutures = catgut = sheepgut. To gut: to hack and slash with a very sharp knife, in the gutting shed. To eviscerate. To fillet. You can do it with a spear. Cut his guts out, like a butcher.

I haven't told anybody this, but the scars embarrass me. That catgut all over your body gets to you after while, makes you sheepish.

4 Those cuts that haven't been sewn just grow together, stick themselves lip to lip, texture for the tissue. Right thigh, about five inches away from doing real damage, a stray skate, heels lower to the ice. A scar about one inch long, a divot. Just below the left thumb, a v-shape, or maybe an L, the long side about one inch

long, fist through a pane of glass early one morning, during a
party. She kissed me under the chin. She came along to be my
party doll.

Tooth, lower jaw, chipped. Al caught me in the middle of a
slap shot, I was watching the puck. O how I love to shoot. You
stride over the blue line and line up your body and glide forward,
driving with your shoulders, puck in front, waiting for the kick of
stick in the ass, the embracing twine. Boom Boom Geoffrion
strikes again.

5   On newly flooded ice, an accelerating skater leaves a string
of oblique stitch marks.

/

\

/

\

/

\

/

The strides open the ice, cut after cut. In typewriting you
call it a slash. Emily speaks of telling the story slant, she knows
how to sing the ice, sign the ayes, the eyes.

The Hockey Fan as Professor

Gene has just moved from Las Vegas. He wants to read the signs. What are those gestures about? He says he really wants to know.

This is SPEARING, I say, tickling his ribs with the point of my stick, and this, I say with a quick spin, is an ELBOW, as I jolt him off balance, and this is a BUTT END, feeling out his solar plexus, and this, turning on my other foot, is SLASHING, whacking him across the knee, and this, as he bends over to catch his shinbone, is a CROSSCHECK, a clean ninety degrees across the back of his neck. And this, I carry him to the armchair, is HOLDING. Have a beer, I say, which he takes and lifts to his lips, but I grab it, INTERFERENCE, I say between swallows. And when you want to learn HIGHSTICKING, BOARDING and CHARGING we'll get skates on.

Rules for a Hockey Story

1　For your starting line choose strong verbs up front with concrete nouns rock-solid on defence.

2　Use proper nouns – quick, quick, slide from one to another – throw the quick pass. Hockey is measured by the speed of the proper nouns, running and running. Pro nouns.

3　All common nouns and adjectives are to be preceded by obscenities which end in "ing."

4　Remember, nonetheless, that hockey is a sweet game and goalies are tender folk.

5　A hockey story is an anatomy. Catalogues, rosters, lineups, histories, biographies, statistics (home and away) are necessary. Include height and weight and scoring records and notes on position, disposition, indisposition. Tell of the time around scars, sprinkle liberally with clichés.There is no tomorrow, the tale has to move quickly. You have to give it all you got to take what you can get.

6　The narrative drives for the goal and the goal is a net framed by steel posts and stuck into the ice, or milk tins or pieces of coal, or the corner of a garage and the garbage can – you know how it goes. The goal of life is. Yes, at the end of it all stands St. As Is, the big stopper. The end. Period.

7 The goal is the key, the goalie key, he keeps it going. The goalie wants the game to go on and on, he does not want you to draw first blood or any blood at all. The goalie is tender, the goalie is quick. He believes in delay. He wants you to try again.

8 Line changes make the game move smoothly. Watch out you don't get caught with too many men on the ice – all those proper nouns piled up in the corner. The ref'll getcha.

9 Shifts are desirable. The quick change of pace catches people up short.

10 You have a choice. You can skate around, throw a deke here, a deke there, a shift and wiggle, turn and hit a body. Bounce around like a soft puck or a bad cheque with no assets. Or you can have tactics. In prose the long line stretches like a poke check right across to the right hand margin, the boards, the tack catches you in the end. You turn a corner every time, like a tic, twitch when you approach the gutter or the edge of things. If you get a chance, slam. Slam him into the boards.

The Hockey Fan Broods Over Spilt Blood

First blood is never stitched or embroidered or carved with hammer and chisel or scratched with a sharp rock or painted or typed or keyed into a word processor, a bloody one blinking on your screen. No, first blood is never given but always is drawn, like at the bank, water from a well, the long rope drips as you haul it up, heavier and heavier to the top.

A blood sport, team sport, teems with sticks and stasis, stops and starts, too-sharp blades throwing snow – a keen game for strapping kids. Sport has strop in it, whets your appetite for steak/roast beef/back bacon/side bacon/front bacon/burnt bacon/ moose meat/flank steak/pot roast/venison/pork roast, ribs, buttons, sweet and sour/chopped up lamb and lamb chops/beef bourgignon/blood sausage, liver, bratwurst/brains/kidney/sheep's head/beef tongue. You know the rest.

How to draw blood. A pool, a puddle, a piddle looks like spilled ink, red or blue. How to draw a puddle. A poodle with a fancy tail and snooty nose and yappy bark. Draw blood with a stick hooked at the end. You bounce one in off your ass and draw blood that way, but the main tool is the stick. St. Ick, patron saint of hockey goons, school principals, snipers, hacks, woodchoppers and lumberjacks, glue factories, backcheckers and shadows. Stay by your man they sing, hold him tight, kick his ankle, stab him in the calf, bellow it out, stay by yer maaaaaaan.

First blood in hockey is different from first blood in bodies. Sometimes first blood is not drawn until the third period. Or overtime. Nothing happens and the zeroes go over time, not under or between the warp and woof but clean over time. No strings attached. Sometimes the game is in overtime before first blood is drawn.

You notice how blood looks clean and fresh when it runs out of somebody else, some other body. The rising flush of surprise. Clean fresh blood makes the 0 into a 1 and you're annoyed and hope for the next game the 0 will stay there behind your kid in goal or above him on the clock and the other team won't draw first, won't draw any blood at all. Keep the warm blood in. He can shut them out cold and the 0 can stand clean beside his name: shutouts 1.

In Genesis the first blood verse says people should not eat other people and should not eat raw meat and should not murder each other.

First blood in the sun-rising morning he was born, she bled and we skoated in the fly, I skoated all the way home like the fifth little piggy, whee whee. Later she sent me to the drugstore. I asked the woman, I couldn't find them and had to ask. She offered to help, rolled her rrrrr's, and I said yes, I wanted napkins, and she rolled her eyes and led me down the aisle. Here you are sirrr, the diapers piled box upon box, how could you miss them. Yes, well you see...my wife...the blood warm in my cheeks. It was blood, her first-born blood, first of the brood, and the blood grew warm in my cheeks.

Tampere to Helsinki

DECEMBER 31 1984 - JANUARY 1 1985   Sunday morning we follow
the paths through the tall pines and over the rocks to the arena
upslope from the hotel. Later, over beer, our Finnish friends give
us the word: "The referees won't let your team win." Our team,
however, plays badly enough to lose without the referee's help.
Despite the loss, Denis is strong in the nets and wins the outstanding player award, a small bronze plate. We have a photo of
Denis holding his award beside the bronze statue of a goalie under
the stands of the upper deck. The bronze goalie wears a bronze
mask to protect himself. He shapes his lips into a spout, his
bronze breath pushed out by the metallic pumping of a bronze
heart. Chug, chug.

Later in the bomb shelter we beat Rockford 6–0. Jared also
strong in goal. Our team has qualified for the championship round,
we're on our way back to Helsinki.

New Year's Eve in the Hotel Presidentii. In the lobby, the
hockey sweaters: Suomi, number one. We're ready to stomp and
shake. Glug, glug, glug. Talk with John Davidson and Don Wittman
of CBC. They covered the World Junior Championship this
afternoon. Canada tied Czechoslovakia 4–4 to clinch the gold
medal. An exciting game, partly because the Finns cheer for the
Czechs.

At the rink the Pin Man shuffles down the corridors, his
jacket heavy with buttons, bronze and silver and gold. Earlier in
the afternoon he was at the hotel lobby, lobbying, quick to say no
to cheap plastic. He has a sharp eye for the expensive metal pins.
Before that he was in the lobby at our game against Toronto. His
hair long and curling up with dirt, he wears a black patch over one
eye, a heavy scowl, dark eyebrows.

The New Year's celebration is a rock-and-roll time, the
band cavorts in coloured lights and smoke. Our travel agent said
Finnish women like to flirt and dance, but they are not on the
make. They are not on the make.

The Hockey Fan Turns the Page

January is the month of Janus/Juno, the patron saints of goalies, janitors and gatekeepers. The goalie keeps it clean in front, struts around the crease, a peacock, wears the mask and looks both ways. He has a horseshoe, they say, a horseshoe all the way up.

The hockey fan glances at the clock, 3:32 and running. Starts up the steps, stays carefully on his own wing, paces the rink. His team trails 2–1. He passes his favourite position near the defensive blue line. He wants to make sure the refs don't miss any offsides. He slows down behind the opposition bench, wants to time it right, just a few seconds, one, two, three rows down, two seats in and the numbers running 1:14, 1:13, 1:12....

January makes a bitter beginning. The Saxons call January Wulf-month. Your teeth rattle and chatter, the wind and air bite wolfishly on the folds of fingers, ears, nose and toes. You need a goalkeeper and a fire to keep the wolf from the door. Yes, to stay fired up you need hot goaltending, first and last, alpha and omega. The cohorts gleaming in purple and gold. Skating on the ice, now.

Helsinki

JANUARY 1-3 1985   My head runneth into the New Year. Eyes and nose outrace the wind, wisps of toilet paper and tissue trail from my pockets. Cough a-roaring. My veins run scotch. Pin Man pushes in front of me to get into the arena, his jacket clinking.

This place is colder than all outdoors. They've caught the drafts from the pack ice cracking across the harbour, gathered every inch of blizzard from the Baltic Sea, stuffed it all into the arena, closed the door and then turned on the refrigeration system. The bleachers are cold, the lobby is cold, the coffee shop is cold, the men's room snaps with frost, the toilet paper scrapes the tender skin of my nose. We lose the game to boot.

WEDNESDAY   A blue cross, I discover, does not signal a drug store. I talk to the people in the store and they talk to me. They use bewildered but concerned looks. I use a variety of coughs and polite sniffing – when they offer me salve for cold sores I know my first efforts were too polite. I gag and snort and rumble. They see, and send me to an apoteeki around the corner. A staff entwined with snakes marks the spot. A young man gives me two bottles of decongestant tablets for about 70 Canadian cents. For the moment I think I will live for the moment.

THURSDAY   Mark and Denis bus to a glass factory north of Tampere. I stay in Helsinki and visit the Finnish National Museum with the Walkers. Yes, his name is John. Later we taxi to the Silya Line dock. Our buses are delayed (Pin Man prowls the waiting room) but eventually we board ship for the overnight trip to Stockholm. I eat and shop duty free, then shower and climb into bed, hardly enough room for my aching head. Dream warm thoughts.

In the dream Lena Grove walks along a road dusted with snow. My, my, she says. A body does get around. In the dream the body gets around steak and milk in the Paddock Restaurant, west then on Portage, west to Brandon a/venue for 5 o'clock nightfall and wheat kings basement of the league, teams piled on the ice whiter than the coach's hair. Her glistening eyes. A Christmas whiteness, the dusty snow. She plaits a dark red loveknot into her long dark hair.

The Coaches Read the Signs

Our goalie has so many letters in his name you can find two alphabets. The letters ride up one side of his sweater, down the other and crisscross in the middle. Nobody knows for sure what his name is so we call him Al for short or Elf 'cause he's little too – dances a sprightly jig in the showers to escape the pontoon-foot guys, quick as a bunny.

But on the ice it's a different story. Al or Elf always slows things down. When he flops on the puck, he makes an alphabet soup and the refs start to read the story on his back and forget to blow the whistle. The other team digs out the puck to score before the refs wake up. It happens every game.

The coaches are going to send Al down. They say he takes too long to get up from the ice. Top-heavy they say. All those letters spell trouble.

A Child's ABC of Hockey

AIR Later you draw water and blood, but first you draw air. Air etches the eardrums, stretches the lungs. Ice is air and water. (Isis is a horny cow.) You chuck snow from your skates into the fire or onto the barrel stove of the skating shack – hissssss until the air runs out, the universe runs down, the verse runs down and you're out of air here, out of ear.

ARENA "A sandy place." Use sand to soak up blood. (Lions 9 – Christians 0.) Push the sand away and get ready for the next batch. In the Winnipeg Arena they take the ice out for the Harlem Globetrotters. We get on the bus, carry our skates and travel to practice in another rink. Like little kids we wear our equipment. At the rink we practice fighting. Get the other guy's jersey over his head and then pummel him. See how they dress, the equipment and weapons. All in array ready to go. "Our array smashes their array," says the Chief Engineer. See Garden.

BORDER CROSSING A guy in uniform climbs on board to find out if we were all born in Canada. Al said he wasn't, he was born in Russia. We start to laugh but the uniform guy bristles. "You get into the office," he says. Al says he is kidding, he was born in England, he digs out his birth certificate. The guy snorts. "No jokes next time," as he steps down the doorwell into a grey sky. "You go too far, I keep the whole bus this side of the line, you go too far."

We had worked for a year to get the Minnesota game, our big road trip for the year, but no fans showed up and the game was dismal. I scored in our own net and got cut on the nose. The return trip was worse. Found out we couldn't buy any beer. We had worked for months to go to the wicked United States and ended up in a dry county. Dry, dry all the way home. Beryl was bored out of her red hair. Even Al was quiet.

DEKE   A quick feint. Drop yr head or tip yr shoulder, then go the other way.

EGGS   Skates as if he has eggs in his pockets, afraid to go into the corners. Skates on eggshells.

FIRE   It all begins around the fire. You hold your hands and toes to the flame, wiggle forward, your back freezes. Melville said we are all drawn to water, to stare into water. So it goes for seaside people, but inland to the north we begin in fire. Some say fire and ice. Yes, as everyone knows, meditation and fire are wedded forever, meditation and ice welded together. A blade and a boot. A lake and a rink.

GARDEN   Eve made a pass and deked Adam into a fig leaf. Now we all start out baby-bum-smooth and get deked out of our jocks and jills. In the gardens. Boston/Madison Square/Maple Leaf. Talked with Peter Gzowski one morning and then walked to Maple Leaf Gardens. A Leaf plays pool with pucks. Or is he curling? He caroms the puck down the ice and then sends another after it, aiming for the face-off circle behind him. The place deserted except for me and people in the stands who sweep the gardens clean. A Leaf alone in the garden.

HOTEL   In the glass-lined bar of the Hotel Presidentii I met a Finn who wanted my address. I said Red Deer was three hours from the Rockies. He said he would stay at my house and visit Banff.

Sunday morning, July 24 1988. Prince Albert, a fine Victorian town. Denis teaches at a goaltending school. He rooms with a German boy who played last year for an Italian team. My hotel window overlooks the highway toward Moose Jaw and Saskatoon.

IDENTITY CRISIS   She breaks in over the blue line and catches me lumbering the other way, flat-footed. Can't use a stick check – she pushed the puck behind me. How to slow down this slip of a girl, this whippet, eyes fastened on the puck as it glides past me. A slim girl with knees up, outskating me to the net. I turn, press my stick on her leg and drop my left arm, then the right, over her shoulders. A comradely gesture – don't use my hands, I just lay on forearms, two arms, and lean a little. Tilt forward with hands out in a palms-up bear gesture, lean and slim on her shoulders. Who me? my hands say. Red hair curls up the back of her neck. She starts to fall and I squeeze my elbows together to hold her. Kiss the top of her white helmet. The puck slides past the goal. The referee whistles. Who me? my hands say with fingers spread. Who me?

JIGGETY JIG   The ice curled up and hauled me into the rut. A huge hole deeper than the open pit hauled me in and crashed me head first into the boards, knocked me cuckoo. And Wayne lugged me home over his shoulder, like a sack of potatoes, we said.

LIE   Any story about a hockey game. The angle of the shaft of a stick relative to the blade bottom when it is flat on the ice. The higher the number, the greater the lie, the sharper the angle. All depends on angles. See sports news. See politician.

LUNCH BUCKET BRIGADE   Grinders, muckers, plumbers, foot soldiers. See cement hands, canoe foot.

MASK   You have to wear one. Grin and wear it, he says, waving his stick like a big scythe. You'll reap rewards later. Grimace and wear it.

NIGHT TRAVEL   Leave after work and head east through Stettler and into Saskatchewan, hug the centre of the road on the cow path between the border and Kerrobert and then north to the Battlefords where the highway widens out, gives room to dodge dead skunks and porcupines. The sun slides down the back window, antelope race parallel to the road. Hockey parents on the road again. Will he play? Will he dress or sit naked in civilian clothes? Can we get there by game time? Before the game is over?

O   A goaltender's dream. The big O.

PONTOON FOOT   Also canoe foot. A big-footed galoot, often with cement hands and cement head. A foot soldier, a defenceman with huge feet and great blocking ability. You judge mothers and hockey players by their feet: little-foot people are fast but have trouble in labour, in the heavy traffic where the pontoon-foot types get by okay. See *The Song of the Stay-at-Home Defenceman*.

PUCK   One who gets passed around.

QUESTION   A matter of degree. Cheer for Alberta teams except when they play Winnipeg, pick Calgary over Edmonton, Canadian teams over American teams, except Philadelphia and sometimes Chicago or Boston, Western teams over Eastern. Muckie mucks.

RIDING THE PINE   Riding the pine means collecting slivers in your ass while you sit on the bench. We had a guy on our team who got drunk because he was riding the pine and who rode the pine because he was always drunk. We dressed him for every game, though, like a turkey for thanksgiving, just because he was so ugly. I forget what position he played on the ice, but we called him our tight end.

SOFT HANDS   The player with soft hands has a touch around the goal, can flip into the upper corner lying down. The touch some call it, the scoring touch. But you need more than soft hands. You need quick feet, the quick eye, peripheral vision, a soft focus and screening, the hard drive in for the score. Takes imagination too, a feel for the game.

SPEAR   See stick, cement head, hack, lumberjack, woodchoppers' ball. Cape Spear, Newfoundland tickles the guts of the Atlantic.

STICK   A long tool curved at one end, comes with variable lies.

SKULL   Spider cracked his skull, but he got up and kept going. Then in the second period he collapsed at centre, rolled around half-conscious. We had to watch he didn't swallow his tongue. They took him to the hospital in an ambulance and were still watching him when I got there. I called Elizabeth. She would drive through the storm, a whiteout. She was a nurse and wanted to look after him. We spoke with Spider, saw webbed blood vessels in the whites of his eyes. He could remember only the first part of the game, how we made a play to score.

"Their centre always tries to shoot the puck forward on the draw," Jack said, "I'm going to let him get the draw. You move toward the boards and he'll shoot it right to you. Then throw it to me up the boards." He did and I did. Spider took the pass and cut around the defenceman, angled in and drove a wrist shot high to the stick side. We didn't score but we got our team going.

Jack put that play together, but he couldn't find the second period at all. Spider quit hockey after that. Walks around with a blank spot, but he remembers that play and I remember too.

TURTLE   Ducks his head, folds his wings over top and slumps down. The other guy pounds thumpety thump on his shell.

WRITING   When they stop on the lake to piss, northern lights dancing overhead, Tom has the advantage. He can finish, underline it, and sometimes, on a warm night, draw a circle, Tom in the centre. But David has trouble. Do you dot the i as you go, or pray for enough pressure to dot it after that last damned painful curving d? Never underestimate the pleasures of a short name.

WISDOM   "Old age and treachery will overcome talent and youth."

ZAMBONI   – You heard about the two Newfies got killed
        icefishing?

   – Noooh, thas too bad. What happened?

   – Got run over by a Zamboni.

   – Aaaaaaaaaaaaaaa.

Stockholm

JANUARY 4–7 1985   We cruise slowly through the archipelago en route to Stockholm. Houses, castle-like in the fog, perch on rocky islands. At the dock we are met by our Swedish hosts from Danderyd, a suburb of Stockholm. Some people call Stockholm the Venice of the North, a city of rivers and canals. Such people dream of the South, but the fogged-in ghost houses say this is Odin's land, the wind crisp and shifty as Odin himself – the trees hang hoarfrost.

We travel to the first church of the region, built circa 1100. A rune stone tells of the people who lived there. The rune a riddle to read. Read me this riddle says I, walking into the wrong washroom. Reading: a fortune-telling. We are guests at a reception and buffet. Smoked salmon and a nice light beer.

The boys go to the Danderyd Klub Hall where they are assigned to their billets. Three games are planned, including one outdoors. Very cold and windy again. Yesterday in Helsinki the wind chill factor was minus 40. It's no warmer here.

I try to phone my Swedish contacts but have no luck. The arrogance of telephones. Boys beat the top team in Stockholm 7–2. Denis outstanding in goal, especially at the beginning and in the last five minutes.

SATURDAY JANUARY 5   Still very cold. Downtown by subway with Mark, Dean and Angela. Over the afternoon we meet most of the boys in one store or another. Boys play their game outdoors against Danderyd. Win 8–1. I nurse my cold: run the shower to fill the room with steam, wash clothes in the bathtub.

Sunday morning our hosts take us to the Needle Tower on the outskirts of the city, past the armed soldiers outside the Soviet and U.S. consulates. From the Needle Tower we see the city laid out below, streaks of gold in the sky. Then we visit City Hall and the Royal Palace.

Outside in the sweeping wind the palace guard changes. Mark gets too close to a guard who makes threatening gestures with his bayonet. Later we see the photo. Mark in his red and white jacket stands at attention, just out of bayonet range, his shoulders drawn up nearly to his ears, hands flat to his thighs in mock formality. Bayonet man looks ridiculous.

After hockey we are taken to a banquet at an old house in Danderyd. I have become addicted to smoked salmon. We drink glüg. Back to the hotel late. Tomorrow night we cruise back to Helsinki on the *Finlandia*.

MONDAY   Our bus tour includes a stop at the Wasa museum, a resurrected 17th century man-of-war lost in the archipelago on her maiden voyage because she was top-heavy. All hands dead. The king insisted on stacking an extra deck to give her more firepower. The ship survived the centuries because she lay, our guide tells us, "where the salt water of the sea meets the sweet water of the river." The Wasa was recovered from the deep in the 1950s, a ghostly galleon, and coated with wax during restoration. Mark and Dean want to visit again, but they misread the bus number and get a ride to the suburbs instead. The houses do look just the same, they say.

The Hockey Fan Goes Cruising

The cruise ship, Stockholm to Helsinki, snuggles into the pier at the bottom of a long runway. Down and down and down the chute we slump, sheep-like, lugging huge wool coats and bags and bags and bags, each lugging three bags full of hockey sweaters and skates, toques and shirts, plastic bread bags, Canadian Club and v.o. (not to mention Johnny Walker Black Label), down and down the chute we carry the bags dancing to our rooms, we dance through dinner, sip goblets of wine, the ship shivering and shifting its way through pack ice, we dance, light on our feet, side step the heavy check of tables and posts, we dance through dinner, humming the old tunes, dance on the floor, laughing I put my hand on her bottom (we're dancing) and she lifts her knee just inside my thighs and nuzzles up, gently, and whispers, *do you like male sopranos*. She did, she said it, just like that and a mean thing it was too considering I had risked a ripping good hernia hauling those bags on board. And she said that to me. Look at her, she's still smiling.

Helsinki to Leningrad

JANUARY 8 1985   We arrive in Helsinki to face another minus 20 wind. All morning we tour the city: Sibelius Park, an underground church, a cooperative housing centre, the cathedral next to the University of Helsinki. On the cathedral grounds a statue built in 1863 honours Czar Alexander II, who allowed the Finns to use their own language. The statue stares mute into the grey sky and snapping wind. The tour guide teaches us a few Finnish words, tells us how to pronounce "sauna" without the nasal honk we give it, the cry of a constipated Canada Goose.

"Excuse me," she says, "but the way you say the word sounds awful to Finnish ears. The word is 'saw ooo na.'"

She tells us too that we should make a point of riding the Leningrad subway, but our enthusiasm pales when she tells how she got lost. We return to the Presidentii for lunch, then stow most of our luggage in the hotel and wait for the airport bus. Everyone is anxious to get on to Leningrad. The Pin Man works the crowd, but we're surly now too and he does little business.

"American aggressif," I hear the man say, or think I hear him say. I am writing this in front of black and white TV news in Leningrad. The newsman has a telephone to his right. The screen images slip by. A demonstration in the snow. A clutch of police. A German shepherd. Meeting of some international committee in Helsinki. Pin Man on the sidewalk, scowling. A glimpse of Bishop Tutu, a voice over a group of black people.

I try the phone system and discover the wake-up call number has been changed. It is not possible to get a wake-up call. I argue, but the operator won't talk to me, she cuts me off and then refuses to answer. In Stockholm, Thomas said the Russians are a great people but have no sense of service. He led us to believe we ought not to expect it. I will sleep forever in the Hotel Pulkovskaya. The telephone as decoration.

Leningrad

JANUARY 9 1985   AM. We drive down Nevsky Prospect, Dostoevsky's street, and view briefly the major buildings of the city: the Winter Palace, the Peter and Paul Fortress, the convent built by Elizabeth, the University of Leningrad, the Admiralty Building, St. Isaac's Cathedral. Our tour shows that Leningrad – St. Petersburg as it was when Dostoevsky gave it this apt description – is an intentional city. Yes, you can see the careful design on every street, the squares and bridges of the old city, although much of the newer city is 1950s box-ugly, new old world, recast after the war and younger than old battle-free Canada.

Tanya, our tour guide, tells us that December Square, site of a bronze statue of Peter the Great on horseback, celebrates the 19th century uprising based on ideas of political freedom gathered from the French bourgeois revolution. She uses the word "bourgeois" several times. Her subtext seems to be that bourgeois political action differs from the people's revolution, that the bourgeois revolutions count, but they count mainly because they made possible the real revolution – the people's revolution that occurred here on the banks of the Neva.

Before that revolution and all its wiles and stratagems, covert and otherwise, Dostoevsky knew what it was to be an underground man. Long before a subway burrowed under the city, he knew undergroundness, for Leningrad, his St. Petersburg, is the natural birthplace of such an idea. If you look around, you see everywhere evidence of the city as a place of deliberate and careful design. And yet, forces opposed to deliberation and design assert themselves. Today one such force is the Russian winter. It is 4:45 PM and nearly dark. At this time of year there are only seven hours of daylight. Since we first landed three days ago in the darkness and drifting snow there has been virtually no sun. The sky has been perpetually hazy with fog drifting in from the Baltic. Such must be the fate of a northerly seaport. The whole city is swaddled and clothed, the citizens wrapped and swaddled in bureaucracy, their voices muffled. They walk the intentional streets under a blanket of fog or snow or mist, or piles of paper.

I think of Mary Shelley's character, Captain Walton, the narrator of *Frankenstein,* how he wrote to his sister of the excitement he felt in St. Petersburg. I think too of the dark consequences of his journey, his meeting on the ice with the strange hulking creature bigger than the biggest defenceman.

Leningrad remains a city of paradoxes, a city of intrigues, of revolution, of great beauty and light and stamina and determination. A city born out of Peter the Great's west-looking vision, born again out of the people's revolution, born again out of the crash and thunder of Nazi bombs. A hero city. The awards she won decorate a civic building, a clock in the centre of its façade, just across St. Isaac's Square from the Cathedral. Tanya stands with her face curled up against the wind, her arm extended, pointing to the memorial banner.

Bomb Threats

In the event of a Bomb Threat at this rink the following procedures shall be followed:

1 The Receipt of a Bomb Threat by Telephone

1.1 The recipient of the call should remain calm, courteous and listen carefully. Do not interrupt the caller, except to prolong conversation. Do not transfer the call. Keep the caller talking. Ask questions: Where is the bomb located? What kind of bomb? Are you a hockey fan? How do you know so much about the bomb? What do you think of Wayne and Janet's baby? Is the bomb in the Rat Room? Do you know the score of tonight's game?

1.2 Make a mental note of any identifiable background noises such as voices, office machines, Zambonis, street traffic, Johnny Cash walking the line, party atmosphere, a woman yelling at kids in the pool hall, the sounds of digging in the potato patch.

1.3 Note distinguishing voice characteristics: loud, soft, high pitch, raspy, intoxicated, professorial, editorial, dictatorial, tory torial, blood-thirsty, drink-thirsty.

1.4 Is speech calm, slow, stuttery, nasal, slurrrrrd, esseterrra?

1.5 Is language excellent or good, fair or foul, better than what the coach says?

1.6 Does the caller have an accent? Grave or acute? Doth the caller lithp?

1.7 Are the caller's manners calm, coherent, emotional, angry, rational, etc.? Estimate the age of the caller.

1.8 Attempt to find out the location of the bomb and identity of person or persons or team to whom the bomb is directed. Is the bomb in the Rat Room?

1.9 Attempt to determine if the person has any knowledge of the building.

1.10 Ask the caller when the bomb is to explode.

2 Immediately After the Call

2.1 Write your mental notes in the space below.

_____

_____

_____

_____

The Hockey Fan Takes Shelter

One of our games was in a bomb shelter ten storeys down into Finnish bedrock. An underground cavern big enough for two ice surfaces, Olympic size, but no bleachers for the fans. Spooky, the ceiling coated with some kind of waterproof stuff, a sparkley white colour – ghost sheets woven with tinsel.

Vending machines guard the stairs, the closed-circuit TV trained on the stairwell and the Pin Man turns and grins, his black eye-patch aimed straight at the camera. The coffee has run out, swallowed up by the fans and the underground rink rats. Our opponents are from Rockford Illinois, west of Chicago. They don't like us and we don't like them. Mark borrows my mitts, he has left his in the hotel. Where I stand, the ice sneaks out under the boards, but I stay there anyway, like a dummy, until the chill works its way up and down from brain to cock to toe. My feet are cold. My hands are cold. Whoever said the centre of the earth was hot? (Warmest place is the men's room, but you can stand around only so long, hands like parentheses cuddling your jewels, before someone thinks you're strange.)

The Garrison Mentality

JULY 24 1988   I visit Fort Carleton this morning, east and north of Duck Lake. Walk the walls, 20 feet up, inspect the fur collection – beaver, bear, ermine, wolf, buffalo, fox, squirrel, skunk. Lift a muzzleloading rifle to my shoulder to zero in on a skunk pelt. The stock about two inches short, built for a 19th century person.

I read the lament of an early factor. The benighted world, he says, thinks pemmican is pounded buffalo meat and bear grease, but he knows pemmican also has hair, skin, dirt, sticks, grass, bits of dung and stones "often of a large size."

A Sunny Day in May

NEWFOUNDLAND TIME

Signs of hockey everywhere. Cape Spear, the easternmost point of North America, slashes out into the Atlantic, used bits of hockey tape flake the snow, the bank huddles in the mouth of the bunker, sunning itself. The big gun, dismantled, with its firing end trained carefully at a concrete abutment, sits on a puck-shaped pad. The salt assault of the sea.

"Holy cow," says Surjit, tapping a Newfie jig on the barrel of the gun, his white turban bobbing against the sky blue all the way to France.

The waves call for an offensive game. Shoooot, they say over and over, shooot shoooooot shooooooooot.

On the way back to St. John's, Dave stops the car on the outskirts of Blackhead. Two teenage girls in bright spring colours walk down the pavement into a seasky of blue and grey, framed by seven or eight houses, cars and trucks, a single scow upside-down in the sun. He makes a rectangle with his hands and holds it at arms-length, focusing. "We could do a painting," Dave says, "Blackhead with Girls."

We turn the corner. A group of young men play hockey on the road. Two fellows lean on a car. Elbows bent they clutch bottles of beer. The pavement ends at the goal. The boys drag their net out of our way, but there is no road ahead, only a stubble of rocks. The goalie has a plastic blade taped onto a shaft. Three shooters, four others look on, wait a turn on the ice, wait for us to get off their asphalt rink.

The Hockey Fan Learns How the World Turns

The proprietor of the sports shop wants to know where ya be from b'y and I tell him Alberta and I ask how he knows we be from somewhere and he says he knows we be from somewhere by the way we hunch our shoulders against the wind when we come in the door and he wonders what our weather be like and we say cold but not like this and he says this is some cold but we gets a warm day wance a year and laughs and he says well, you know b'y there's a reason for the bad wedder. You know we been takin' all the oil and gas from Saudee Arabee for years and years and things are getting lopsided. We let the gas out by the tonne in one place and then make all this havvy smoke over on this side, factories and such, and things get worse, letting off over there and pushing down over here. Like a basketball, he says, like that basketball the Harlem Globetrotters have, you know, they t'row it down and it bounces back this away or that away, 'cause it has a weight on one side, ya see, off balance and you never knows which way it's goin' to bounce. Like the wedder, ya see b'y?

On the plane back to Toronto, the b'y reads how E.J. Pratt was confirmed in Blackhead years before he chased the Red Deer woman. This is true, you can look it up.

Leningrad

JANUARY 10–11 1985 "Maybe Canadians don't think it is cold?" Tanya has just told us that there is more snow this year than usual. It is also colder. But maybe to us it is not cold? We snort and rumble that this is plenty cold, attempt to tell her of the warming chinooks, the delights of an Alberta winter.

We go downtown to visit the ethnic history museum. The temperature this AM is minus 16 with a sharp wind blowing through the squares. A busy city moves its snow, much of it pushed by hand, women in their 50s and 60s. Someone asks why grandmothers are working at labouring jobs. Tanya says, "O they are peasants."

This is no dictatorship of the proletariat. For Dostoevsky it was a city of many bureaucrats, and it still is. You can walk down Nevsky Prospect and find them, buttons bristling.

Later we are treated very well at the hockey game, but the game is no contest. The coaches were told our opposition would be boys 13 and 14, as ours are. The Russian boys, though, look to be 12 and one rumour says some of the Leningrad boys are 11.

Nevertheless, many good things happen. Jan is regaled with sandwiches and cognac which materialize from under a Russian woman's fur coat. Three young men offer me warm red wine. A tumbler full of the warm south, beaded bubbles winking at the brim.

On our return to the hotel, we talk with the doorman. He's a jolly sort. We talk to him, obliquely, by relaying questions through a woman in our group who speaks Ukrainian. We ask about one of the pins he wears on his lapel. He beams and tells us it's a medal he was awarded for track and field as a youth. Another uniformed and buttoned man, not so jolly, sends the doorman back to tend the entrance.

THURSDAY.   We visit the Winter Palace and the Hermitage, and in the evening go to a ballet called "Czar Boris." How to catch the fullness of the day. To walk across the square of the Winter Palace, tour the Hermitage and view in a single gallery not one but 25 Rembrandts, parade through gallery after gallery – da Vinci, Titian, the Italian masters, the Spanish, a Michelangelo sculpture, dozens of Impressionist works. To stop in the hall overlooking the Neva, the 18th century English clock, gold leaf birds and squirrels brilliant in the filtered midday light. To look over the snowbanked garden which once was the skating rink of Catherine the Great. These events do not easily translate. They create a thick lust, an erotic edge that the evening ballet only caresses warm and warmer.

The Russians have a word to describe such experience: transliterated as "ostraneniye," it means making strange, some say defamiliarization. The purpose of art is to slow down perception, to make the familiar new again, to make the stone stony. The word was coined by a Petersburg scholar, Victor Shklovsky. Now, for me, a Leningrad word. The transport that art brings. Jouissance. Coming.

In the evening we go to the hotel bar. The uniforms here suggest some patrons are seamen, others airline pilots. People love to dance and cavort whether or not they have partners. The band plays three or four rock songs in a set and then disappears for a huge stretch of time. They seem more often on break than on duty. We drink our cognac. Then we discover that the dance band must have been hatching something on their breaks, for later in the evening, in the city where the concept of defamiliarization was born, where Captain Walton launched himself over the snow to find Frankenstein, where Dostoevsky discovered the underground man, where Lenin and his people reshaped the modern world – in such a city this band plays the Bird Dance. With all the snaps, flaps and wiggles. O no/o yes/o no/o yes.

The Hockey Fan in Love Again
A Romance

He snuggles into the seat of his big red Thunderbird. She gives him that little smile, you know the kind, and her eyes sparkle as she wiggles her bottom and pulls the seatbelt over her leopardskin coat. The hockey fan thinks the coat a little too jungle-ish for the Canadian prairies north of the 52nd parallel, but he likes her smile and her eyes and the way the belt fits tight across her breasts. He runs the car up to speed, flips on the radio, hums a little tune. Clicks on the cruise control. His voice on the radio? Yes, yes he has found himself on the radio. He hears himself on the radio, talking. Even as he looks at the woman beside him he hears himself talking.

Without consulting us, the coat gives Jane her name. I don't blame you for it; leopardskin does that. But the consequences chuff along behind the adjective. You nestle Jane into a viney bower, finger wildflowers into her hair, silky twists above her ear; you imagine him as a chest-beater, a hairy Tarzan stuck for words except when he talks to animals, his call as charming as the groans of a constipated bull-ape. I'm not blaming you – adjectives do these things. Give them a noun and they take a story.

We can change it. She pulls the seat belt over her coat – just hack out the leopardskin. A quick flick of the delete button. But now you have an unobservant character: it's as if he looks at her but doesn't see what she's wearing. A trifle risqué for so early in the story, so for the sake of decorum, we stay with the leopardskin coat and cover her up with the name Jane. This is a romance with the usual décor.

Jane drives to the airport with the hockey fan, sparks sprinkle and fly, they fall in love: a simple tale complicated only by the coat and perhaps by the tiny birthmark on Jane's cheek just above the crinkle she makes when she smiles.

And by the radio. Singing in the wilderness, his voice between the characters, fills the available space. "Hockey is a war game."

He's hairy but his paunch doesn't look like Tarzan's ironing board belly. And the setting is no wilderness. He turns past the stand of poplars at the bottom of Antler Hill. The poplars are as tall as trees in a romance. Horse ranches on both sides of the highway. You can see the drilling rig. No apes or leopards, no bellow or snarl of jungle cats, no saliva drips from bared incisors, but if you listen you hear the saliva slip between radio teeth. Some static. The magic number three has imprinted itself in the modern consciousness. Heavy stuff for a romance, but you see he's not Tarzan. The sign nailed in the dressing room, "Take up our quarrel with the foe, to you from failing hands we throw," in English and French.

Quotation marks whistle and curve through saliva-soaked teeth. A gravel sound: good, washed gravel.

At the margin a realistic story niggles. Animal snarls and curled upper lips. Tongues on teeth. Lust for the fair body wrapped in (leopard) skin. Eye teeth. Watching you and the ferocious coat.

Guts squiggle and crinkle, but she's safe. Hurtling down the highway, speed limit 110 KM per hour, he listens to the radio voice and watches for blowouts or blizzards or crazies racing down the wrong side of the road, three-ton trucks spilling bibles. He has his hands tied, so to speak. She snuggles into her coat, her seat bucket, the safety belt. Marginal dangers: fleshy tangles, here a limb, there an organ, rubbing together. You have noticed, though, as he has, that roads lead from this highway into shaded nooks – clumps of poplar, birch and spruce to be exact – but a man in a car with Jane is likely to think of nooks, and in a romance they are always shady.

You knew from the moment she smiled. As soon as he shoved into his seat.

The hockey fan cruises up Antler Hill with Jane in her coat, his eye cocked for road hazards, ear perked to the radio, straining to hear her every move. What should he do? Listen to himself talk? Turn himself off and talk directly to her? Light banter? Shady nooks demand light banter. Or smile his casual smile and let her hear his voice offer wisdom to the world. Puff out his chest, suck in his paunch. He could ask, he does ask himself, how it would seem if he put his arm across the top of her seat. Horns of a dilemma.

He searches for a clue, hears himself say a voice from the dead is an essential device of World War I poetry and in the dressing room of the Habs hang the lines from "In Flanders Field." He tries to read her smile, her lips are red, not like roses, like poppies, we could say. He lifts his hand. She folds her arms across her chest.

The forward pass, usually delivered with the wrist, forehand or backhand, the back pass, the carom or bank pass, the flip pass, the blind pass, the suicide pass, keep your head up, the two-line pass, the offside pass, the offhand casual and inadvertent pass glances off the skate, the leg, the bum, the arm. Not the casual lazy boneheaded pass? Yes, the lazy casual bonehead pass, yes and the quick pass, O for a roll in the soft, soft snow, quickly/a coolie, the mountain pass with and without avalanche, the bare pass, the warm wet snow, the passing bell, the passion pass, the passing show en passant, pass it off, pass it up. Throw the puck, which in your case you have not got. Up the boards.

The first big test:

She says she wants to hear the radio program.

Or since you think he's heavy-handed and brutish she says she wants to listen to music. Wang dang doo, dabbeee dabbee doo.

He's stung. But he knows where he stands as the car pulls to the top of Antler Hill. He knows how to read her folded arms. She's aloof, not defensive or hostile, but resistant to his charm, challenging him. A polite smile. Waaah waaah dooo.

In a romance the technicolour setting turns the hard-hearted heroine into butter. Fields stretch to the horizon, the mountains are jagged shadows behind a curtain of warm grey clouds. The town right-angled and sharp-edged, a bulbous water tower, spider-legged. To the east twin silos stand firm. Anthony Henday saw the Rockies from this hill, the first white man to see the shining mountains. Trumpets and cymbals. *Dulce et decorum est.*

Or she says nothing. She just smiles. Raises her eyebrows and smiles, her beauty mark moves a touch but she says nothing. A neat bit of stickhandling, her silence. They pass Innisfail. Graders and bulldozers and earth-moving machines trundle across the landscape. Tension. Metaphors. The whole works.

The machines in the garden ruffle your feelings. They are figures for disruption, unearthing, noise. Like Jane's silence, these machines evoke the spoiled moment – the dropped ice cream cone, the lion pissing on you at the zoo, the computer glitch, disconnected sentence chunks folded between paragraphs, slogging in the trenches, a lover's rubbery indifference.

Especially when she puts her hand on his. The hockey fan has his right hand on the seat. Drives with his left, the car in cruise, at 113 KM per hour. He speeds only modestly, he is a modest man. Then she puts her other hand on his. He tells how the comitatus signifies a siege mentality and how it rises up in adolescence and other times of stress. "They bunch up." He looks at the road, at her. Her hands linger warm on his fingers. He thinks nooks and crannies.

The touch could be, to you from failing hands, a gesture of friendship. I will listen to the radio if you want. I like you, therefore I touch your hand. I'm here, therefore you are. But she says nothing, she just smiles.

Into the hollow between Innisfail and Bowden, past the jail, the police dog training gymnasium on the left, to the right the gas refinery. Flags flap in the wind. South south-west. She has him in her web, she has outsmarted him. How soft her skin to kiss, to touch. Her lips poppy red describe an arc, petals on a flower. He wants to run his fingers gently up the nape of her neck, which he cannot see and you cannot see, hidden so by her golden tresses.

Her hair is actually dark brown and knotted in crinky little curls, dunnish at the roots if you get close enough, but golden tresses go with the light banter and shady nooks, and they help to push the grapple-and-puff fantasies to the gutter where they belong. A chaste kiss or two may be appropriate, this is a romance, as long as you remember the characters are cardboard and do not have insides that gurgle and squeak. The characters do wiggle of course. We made them wiggle at the beginning to give the cardboard some snap, but don't forget she's wearing her leopardskin coat and he's listening to himself on the radio. She smiles at him, her lips poppy-red. Pasted in a smile. Hair grey at the roots.

In the dark romance a femme with fatale hair, tongue on the corner of her mouth, tempts a fresh young man to his doom. Catches him in her net. The torch is a symbol of light. In the pastoral romance the heroine has golden tresses. And a pretty smile. Don't let the coat fool you. Web and spider echo the prison image I stuck into the landscape you are driving through. Fairy tales and romances require links between situation and character. The clock strikes twelve and Cinderella is transformed. The hockey fan feels trapped. "Hemmed in your own zone," he says. "The torch is fire and all things that rise into the heavenly dome *dum de do be dum* get you up for the game, all fired up."

Tantalizing fingers on his zing, zing thigh. I use the synecdoche because he and she are modest. They sit primly in the Thunderbird humming down the highway. A fine touch she has, such hands. Jane in a leopardskin, a fine winter day, driving to the airport. The best of all possible worlds. And the radio tells how they clear the zone.

Just a little bit closer she smiles, and runs her hand higher, tugs his belt loose, pushes inside to keep her hands warm, only that. The radio voice says there's no tomorrow.

Peacefully down the highway at 113 KM per hour. She smiles at him, yes she does have her hand on his. Yes, she moves her hand a little, yes. A smile on her face. She says the magic words three times, backwards, you're my kinda man. Or she points to her grandmother's farmhouse. See the red trim on white, rooted in canola just beyond those mounds of dug-up highway. The jagged lines of trenches. The Calgary tower noses up the horizon.

Just whacked a hunk out of time and space. They're closing in on the airport. You don't need every foot of pavement or the sign painted in dayglow orange on the side of the wrecked greenhouse, "Bonjour Tory Traitors." You don't need these details, · this is a romance. In hockey you fight for space, every inch, he says, you give it all you've got to take what you can get.

She forgot her basket of bananas. He goosed back and forth on vines in the hotel jungle, washboard belly rippling in the breeze. She feels sheepish. If she asks him to stop at her grandmother's house, he will think she is scatterbrained – pretty enough but skittery. Makes appointments and then gets lost. Says who who when she means he he. Leaves her bananas in hotel jungles. Her golden tresses disappear. He sees her dark brown hair.

She fingers the buttons of his shirt. It could happen. The voice drones on, she nibbles the tip of his chin, she hums too, the last button, the last bar. She hasn't said a word, the voice tells how hockey players get caught up in male fantasies, race around with sticks and drive powerful cars to escape the pursuing puck bunnies, tails twitching. Nails slide down his belly. The myth of the crucified Canadian, nails just touching belly hairs, they band together to loot and plunder at night. Underground thieves and vagabonds. Her coat slips, falls from her shoulder. Silk lining, red lines with white circles. Face-off.

Her right index finger outlines his belly button, she tickles his nipple with her tongue, right nipple, the T-Bird hums along. Assonance and consonance.

The prose romance is characterized by an isolated setting, characters simplified or larger than life, swinging on the vine, dreams or fantasy or nightmare qualities, the pursuit of an ideal. Heaves the coat into the back seat. His grail runneth over.

And if the pass does not connect you have still cleared the zone, the drop pass needs a light touch and is usually delivered in the offensive zone, the drop pass is designed to set up a scoring play, the player with the puck crosses the line, then drops the pass to the teammate who follows her, you make the puck stop while you're moving forward at a quick pace, use a soft touch.

The microwave tower is painted red and white. Like the stacks on the gas plant, three stacks high, red and white candy stripes with the smell of rotten eggs. The grandmother, hunched on her yellow pillow in the little white and red house, has false teeth, piano keys. Hates bananas and washboards. Had enough of them when yer ma was a gaffer.

Do watcha do to me, *doo doo* strums his lobe and thumbs the elastic. Stitches grow tighter and, yes, wait for the opening, the gap, the quick pass and then she cups his arm across the legs, the cruise control, the T-Bird humming. Be yours to hold it high. The rest is not there, a continuous phrase, a slight pause after yours and it. Be yours to hold it high, but he goes on speaking, If ye break faith with us who die, we shall not sleep, the two long open vowels stressed, though poppies blooooooow.

SLOW DOWN NOW a sign on #2 Highway. The Mounties lurk behind that earthmover. The thrill of combat, the power of the comitatus, the noble selfless feeling of giving yourself to protect your buddies, a sense of cameraderie they say, esprit de corps, they say, chemistry, team play, male bonding. The Calgary tower erect on the horizon lifts its flame, a torch in the dotted sky, the torch held high. The language of victory. To blow out, slaughter, wipe out, romp through, demolish, blast, whitewash, hammer, to skunk (it could happen), we walked away with it, we just killed them.

Nothing but a boys' game people say, the unmentionable salaries, just men playing a boys' game. They stand up to be counted, a close-knit group sewn together. Stitch, stitch, stitch.

The bird hums over the torch held high, they are right over the tower, her golden tresses pink in the flame-light, they fly, humming, flushed in their thick embrace, scarce heard amid the guns below, the humming bird a tight fit ooo they fly up into the dancing blue/red/green/yellow shimmy of the aurora dancing into the embrace of the night sky, they slide through the red flame over Mars, you remember eye teeth humming on the edge, glide towards Venus, golden in the night over the flaming tower, you know how it goes – they fly, they fly.

Another Story of Love and Affection

You hear hockey players brag about how tough things were when they were kids skating on outdoor rinks, as if no one else played in the winter. In fact, snow stories have a long history. On his way back from Xanadu, Marco Polo travelled through the snows of Russia. Polo and a friend wrote the travel stories from prison in 1300 or so, counting the time. Polo and his friend say that in Russia drinking parties go on all day, summer and winter. During these day-long parties the ladies stay in their places and "their handmaids contrive to give them relief unobserved, when need arises, with the aid of large sponges." He goes on to tell how on a particularly fierce winter day after such an all-out binge one lady squatted in the grass and got herself frozen to the ground. She yelled out in pain and her husband came to her aid. He was himself reeling drunk. To help her, he stooped over and blew on her, hoping to set her free with the warmth of his breath. A delicate position. "But while he breathed," the translator says Polo says, "the moisture of his breath congealed and so the hair of his beard froze together with his wife's and he too was stuck there unable to move for pain." They couldn't budge until others came to help them break the ice.

Hockey Night in Leningrad

Tonight the boys play outdoors. We bundle up and hustle past the grinning snowman in the foyer, line up for the buses, trying to remember which one smells of diesel fumes and which one is okay. I wear my Leningrad overshoes: one sock, one bread bag, another sock, another bread bag. Warmest my feet have been since we landed in Helsinki two weeks ago. The night is frosty and festive, steamed-up windows filter city lights.

This game is the hockey highlight of the tour (tomorrow we go to the ballet, Friday to the circus). We know they will pull all sorts of crooked tricks to beat us. The favourite scenario has it that each period they will ice a different and more experienced team than the last, saving their national team for the third. This is serious. In Finland the home crowd had a special chant especially for our fans. "Go Canada Go," the Canucks shouted. "Go Canada Go Home," the Finns shouted, as if we were Americans or something. And if the Finns didn't like us, and they're supposed to be on our side, imagine what these guys will do. Shave off whiskers, hunch down into their boots to look like thirteen- year-old kids, stick Tretiak into goal, anything to wipe out the rotten capitalist Canadians.

At the sports centre the flags are straight out, the temperature is minus 20 Celsius. A crowd has gathered and they gawk politely as we are directed into the hall to get warm. We are eighteen hockey players and thirty mothers and fathers and sisters and grandmothers and friends. We share the warm hall with a few hockey officials, trade some pins and buttons.

Outside in the wind people are packed four or five deep around the rink. There must be three hundred here, shifting, stomping, breaths fogging the soft fluffy snow. This is a community sports centre sponsored by Aeroflot, big letters painted on the boards. Red and white and orange we weave into a dark field of fur hats and warm coats. I stamp my feet.

"Fred."

A tug at my sleeve. I have to turn my whole body, my hood is up and I can't see past the fur.

"Fred. You want a drink?" A young man in his twenties. He's talking to me.

"Yes," I say, "vodka?"

"No," he says, "vino."

We walk to his two companions, one of whom has a bottle tucked under his coat. He hands me a tumbler, pours it full. We lift glasses in salute. The wine is warm and good.

The second man lights a cigarette. I offer my pack.

"American, Salem Menthol," says the first man and takes one, proud of his English.

"My sons," I say pointing to Mark and Denis, who stand together behind the screen. Denis still wears the top half of his goal equipment. He has just finished his turn (we're now leading 8 to nothing) and he has been quick to get off his skates and back out into the cold. He looks incredibly puff-bellied and skinny-legged, his orange hockey sweater trimmed with blue, a Canadian flag on his sleeve. He looks like a strange exotic bird who landed here by mistake. Mark too an odd creature in red jacket with white sleeves, huge leather mitts, a purple-coloured camera bag on his belly, and grey Russian fur hat, a coup made earlier on the street near the Winter Palace. Together the boys define motley.

As we light cigarettes, a hand pokes in front of me. I am being offered coins. I shake my head. My friend Fred says, "Nyet, nyet, no beesiness here." We smoke and thank each other as the crowd noise picks up. The Russian boys attack our goal but leave themselves open on defence and we break away only to be foiled by their goaltender. An exciting moment. I turn to my comrades but they have disappeared and my feet are getting cold.

In the hall a man gives us postcard pictures of the city. He explains by gesturing with his palms down that the gifts are from the boys on the hockey team. In return he accepts bubble gum. We are invited into our team's dressing room. Two tables standing end to end are spread with pastries and rolls. A giant silver urn of tea shines buddha-like in the corner.

Outside in the wind the goals add up. The Russian boys finally score. The crowd cheers. The wine bottle is gone.

My belly is warm.

Leningrad

JANUARY 11 1985   "Yah cold, damned cold." The woman at the
door smiles and laughs, pleased with her English and pleased that
we are pleased. "Damned cold, yah cold."

The wind slams us as we parade past a line of Russians
and into St. Isaac's Cathedral. We are being given preference,
though I'm not sure why. The Russians have been waiting at least
the fifteen minutes it has taken our two buses to unload. They
stare at us and a strange group we are. Most boys and men have
sprouted Russian fur hats. These are worn with our blue leather
coats, red and white hockey jackets, and multi-coloured parkas
and scarves. Ahead of me in our line, Mark wears his grey fur hat
with the flaps down. He has been regarded as a swap artist since
he first traded his toque for the fur hat. The rate of exchange
floats. Today Dean got a fur hat for two baseball caps.

We enter the Cathedral for the first time, though we came
to St. Isaac's square on the day we landed in the city. Inside, St.
Isaac's is a monument of signs, a boggling set of contradictions.
The religious icons and furniture have been lovingly restored,
mahogany panels, stained glass, lapus lazuli. Yet in the very centre
of the cathedral, swinging from its central dome, is Foucault's pendulum. Russia's old battle with mediaeval values carries into the
present. So too does the Second World War, evident in the ongoing
reconstruction of the external façade.

Edmund Wilson found St. Isaac's "Byzantine and creepy,
anti-religious exhibit creepy too...." The cathedral is not creepy
now – the Peter and Paul Fortress is creepy. All those Czars buried
there under foot, the darkness, the butts and elbows of people
milling. The icons and stained glass and polished wood make the
cathedral stunningly beautiful.

Tanya emphasizes the research and "scientific" work done to restore the building, the process of the original construction. "This cathedral is a monument not only to the architect," she says, "but to the working people who built it. The man who made this scale model without a single nail was a serf, but he entered the competition and was given his freedom." The model precedes the story. Art is delay, a stalling tactic, like the pick play in hockey. Makes you look again or think again, see the church in the cathedral.

An attendant, lean and unsmiling, scurries from one scold to another. Edmund Wilson does not mention the attendants inside or the damage outside. The shell holes had not been delivered then. In 1935, their time had not yet come.

Playing Time Is a Fiction

He thinks of playing time. I need playing time, he says, I need the time coach, I need the ice time. Playing. Ice time is the thing wherein I'll catch the fancy of the queen. Ice is the thing he says. I sing the puck.

On the other hand. Playing time does not equal real time. Play time is the gap between clock time and game time.

And then of course. Hockey turns on the number three, beginning, middle and end, delayed sometimes but an end nonetheless, often a modest closure, a tie, like kissing your sister. If you go into overtime you have sudden death or sudden victory. Either way there's no tomorrow, they say. And what's wrong with kissing your sister?

But still. Clock time is ten seconds of silence before the beginning of the long dash.

Even though. At this very moment an island floats slowly across the Canadian Arctic. Within twenty years it will be in the United States and then later in the Soviet Union, floating all the time.

Scouting Report: Floats around centre ice. Leaves a big gap between himself and the dee. Spreads his legs like that and sooner or later he'll get a kick between the big toes with a frozen snowshoe.

Nevertheless. Playing time is a fiction. He likes to play, play it out, string it out more and more. Until a period gets in the way, breaking time though he tries to play right through, and in the end he wheezes after each shift. Gobs of phlegm rattle in his throat. His ass droops and his belly sags but he keeps going. Tells himself he can go again but time catches up anyway. We all get it in the end. One scything sweep check stops you cold or the big butt end knocks you tits up, suckers skyward and they put you on ice.

But as I said before. In the middle fiction is play time and outside the rink, off ice, the universe winds down or winds up, stretches and delivers. Ozone breaks down or builds up. Great streams of gases shoot off our galaxy, they say, people molest each other in the usual ways, the Middle East is middling quiet for the Middle East, bibliothumpers browbeat and harangue, bully bash and murder in the name of right, people everywhere duck the dentist, pay the piper, shake the social worker, badger the butcher, kick the cat. The sun groans after last night's shaker and comes with a great noisy crack. A head-splitting dawn spilling too bright for words spells HANGOVER in braille on the wet side of your eyelids. Still, bellybuttons collect lint, stains colour your lover's underwear, glass shatters in the street, socks get lost in the dryer. And, in spite of the strides of regimentation and definition, the galaxy hurtles along, a stitch in time, while love is no more gentle than it should be and scotch whiskey, my love, amber warm in the goblet, makes its way overseas for the betterment of humankind and the ease of mid-life crises, both yours and mine.

Neat is it. Take it neat? Want some ice?

He said.

Moreover.

From Notes Written Over the Polar Seas

In the afternoon of our fourth day, we visit the museum of Russian art. Splendid portraits of Tolstoy including one showing him in his peasant pose, with bare feet. I ask if there are portraits of Dostoevsky. She prefers to talk about Tolstoy.

Some of the landscapes show the breadth and sweep of the steppes. There is no Chagall here, the collection is overwhelmingly representational. One of the most striking works is by Tolstoy's friend, Ilya Repin. The painting, called in English "Zaporozh Cossacks Drafting a Reply to the Turkish Sultan," shows men clumped around a table. Shaved heads with topknots, some fur hats, curving mustaches, full grey beards. Bare teeth, chests full, chins up. They are laughing. At the table sits their leader, their literary leader, with a quill pen. Poised above paper. Just in front of him is an inkpot. The writer is framed by two pipe smokers. He is laughing and the men around him, some of them naked to the waist, are laughing too. These are not ironic laughs but full-bellied explosions. One of the half-naked men holds his sides as if to emphasize the point. Others have their heads tilted back. Their laughing and smoking, in- and out-bursts of breath, play against the formality of the writing. Perhaps writing itself causes the laughter.

The men are drafting a reply to the sultan who has ordered them to surrender. Booming laughter, a huge collective toe-tickling guffaw is their reply (the painting a replay), the letter a ritual gesture. Altogether the painting suggests vigour and power and joy and cameraderie, delights of shared response.

On our last evening in the city we visit the Leningrad circus. Outside, a man waves a blowtorch under his bus, lovers arm in arm nuzzle in the light clean snow. Inside, the building smells of urine, stale and fresh and stale. Smoking is confined to the washrooms, where a sweet Turkish tobacco and sewer stench make a nasal delight.

During the performance Russ falls asleep in his chair, his mouth wide open. A clown heaves a ball up into the second tier. The ball arcs towards Russ's snoring jaws but misses. Jared kicks the ball back, it bounces wildly and sends the clown tumbling and falling over himself, cartwheel after cartwheel. The people laugh.

All manner of creatures chase each other around the ring. A baby moose, dogs, a porcupine, a bear, a pig, a rooster. Mark says, "Where is the skunk, I bet they won't send out a skunk." He's right, though they do send matched horses.

Après-circus we drink cognac and champagne in the bar. Dance too, chase each other in a ring.

The Hockey Fan Hits Middle Age

When I came home I found out she had put my skates in a garage sale. We don't even have a garage. Those skates had no blade left so I suppose they got thrown out, like garbage, as if they were worthless. I liked those skates. Pro's and Tacks, the best you could buy in Bell's Hardware in 1960. The boots were short – you had to sew on your own tendon guards – and made of leather, not that rubber and plastic crap they try to pass off for skate boots now. And the blades were steel too. Just steel – not clear plastic or blue plastic or white plastic. All steel. And none of those wimpy rubber nibs on the tip of the heel. Made good weapons, those skates. I got one in the head once but I've never seen the scar since I quit wearing a brush cut. Have long thick hair now and long slender eyelashes. And a pair of skates made of nylon, each with a little rubber tip on the heel of the blade.

The Hockey Fan Goes Reading

SASKATOON JANUARY 15   Minus 30 degrees Celsius. Cars grind out clouds of exhausted smoke, bundles of scarves and mittens and fur hoods swaddle down the sidewalk, the snow squeaks under foot. A sharp snap in your lungs. Snow snakes slither across the road.

The hockey fan hustles through the painted doors into the warmth of Kelsey Tech. He is going to give a reading. He circles the corridors sipping hot tea. Students have prepared posters. One shows a dumpy little hockey player wearing his photograph for a head with "Birk" on the front of his jersey. He is round and unhockey-like. (I am smiling stupidly at Elaine. She took the photo. You can't see her but I can.)

Another poster is a collage. A red plastic puck sliced in half and glued on the poster sticks out at you. In the centre a photo of Wendel Clark in his Maple Leaf jersey, big letters at the bottom: "Wendel Clark is not coming, but Birk Sproxton is." The hockey fan riding, riding over the driven snow.

He sucks his tea and rehearses the reading. His potato story, the exquisitely crafted lyrics about midnight swims at Phantom Lake, the wonderful song about writing names in the snow. Love poems? He will read love poems.

Michael begins the introductions. In the front row a man wears a Saskatoon Blades cap. Michael tells how Denis plays for the Prince Albert Raiders. The Blades hate the Raiders and the Raiders loathe the Blades. The hockey fan hears the slash of swords, cannon blasts, crosschecked skulls and bones crunching. A pistol waves in his face. The man in the front row smiles, hand inside his coat.

The reading begins.

A STORY LIKE A SHOVEL

They are eating fish and chips. It's his birthday. He's forty-seven and looks it.

Here's your present, she says.

It's a book. "Moving Out," the letters on the cover look like squeezed red toothpaste flecked with coconut (which has enough good sense to grow in the sun). "Moving Out" tells you everything you want to know about getting your own place. How to pick roommates, how to budget, how to build a fish farm, how to grow potatoes. Flowering reds that burst into splendid white blossoms.

And take your shovel with you.

The girl in the supermarket has pretty breasts, wears a fishnet shirt, little holes held together by pieces of string. Netted gems, he thinks, ruby red.

She makes him take off his shoes and leave the shovel at the door.

You're the apple of my eye, he sings, nipples like rose buds, lips like cherry wine...

She lifts her cabbage leaf.

This garden talk will get you nowhere. How can you have potatoes if they don't flower? We have acres and acres of potato tops with no bottoms.

I don't know, but the potatoes are there, I dug them out with my own fingers, the proof is on the plate. Red potatoes, right in front of your nose.

She lifts both arms, rolling the white and black stripes of her blouse.

I don't believe it, potatoes cannot grow without flowers, the seed potatoes we planted are fruitless things, all tops and no fruit. You should have fed them horse manure.

Our potatoes are not in acres, they are in patches, three hills under the weeping birch – weeping I suppose because the potatoes didn't flower – and three hills do not an acre make. The potatoes are there, I fish around under the plant, dig them up with my fingers. I have mud on my white bucks, mud under my fingernails. The shovel shivers at my touch as if I had caught leprosy or potato blight.

I believe in flowers. I don't see how they could grow if they don't have flowers, she says, eating the delicate white pickerel. Red teeth flecked with bits of fine white pickerel.

She lifts her eyebrows.

(A potato is a potato, the tales now go, says Frost with a smile, ladder over his shoulder. Potato peels make good fences.)

In the dream an undulant walk to lie in the sun warm beside the river. Plunging into shivering flower blossoms and tail flipping fish striped black and white and red in golden water, shimmering circles in moonglow night, fingers circling under warm wet potato flesh.

In the dream they always eat afterwards, shovel lying across the bed.

A champagne breakfast. She's dressed in white, a fluffy ruff rings her neck, white, like potato flowers. Her sharp teeth bite the once-red potatoes, fluffed and mushed by the chef's potato musher and dressed with sour cream. She rolls her tongue over the bite on her fork and says since he spends all his time with plants he should find an acreage somewhere and leave her with her fine red skin and pouty white lips to cultivate men who know enough of women to keep fingernails and white bucks clean.

Anyway, everybody knows that potatoes have flowers.

You're a peach, he says.

———————

Fingernails still dirty, grime ground in up to the cuticle and invading the blood stream, colouring the rich red Canadian blood, a delicious concoction of English, Pennsylvania Dutch, French-Canadian, Irish and Indian (one of the Algonkian-speaking tribes, Algonkian speakers they were, words finely edged as imagist poems). The potato grime turns blood the colour of a goldeye from the Red River or the Red Deer River (Alberta or Manitoba, take your pick) or a redeye from the River of Golden Dreams at high flood, precious and reddish, carrying acres of golden potatoes down the long filter of a rumble belly potato tube.

———————

I'm going to buy my potatoes at the supermarket where you can see them grow right before your eyes. Potatoes were made to be grown in supermarkets.

The bloom is off the potato, she says, flaunting striped pants and white sports coat.

Besides that, you snore.

———————

I consult M. Foucault. He digs the garden. Pommes de terre, he says, I don't mess with potatoes, I go for coconuts and red toothpaste. I am planting the toothpaste seeds now and watering them. You should see them, they always flower before the tubes appear.

He hands me a pink carnation, goes great with my white bucks.

———————

In the kitchen making perogies, thinking of shovel jokes. He folds the pastry over his first two fingers and then spreads them into a v. Spoons in fleshy potatoes and sews it shut, neatly, with suture thread left over from Frankenstein movies or from last night's hockey game. He sews the potato perogies shut, like little gobs of pemmican, puts them carefully into the fridge behind the apple.

––––––––––

Dreams of the supermarket girl, climbing ladders with her, who goes first? she laughs tickling his knackers with the shovel handle. So you want a couple of acres? Hee, hee, giggling among the smoked goldeye. Swimming and thrashing, tickling water, visions of arks, two by two, hands together, paddle the ladder together, hands and feet, sixty-nine strokes per side, then switch, canoeing a garden, the warm wet rain.

Winnipeg goldeye. Eyes flashing.

––––––––––

(The potatoes flowered in the night and were killed by frost. Something there is that doesn't love a potato.)

––––––––––

The supermarket girl orders roast pork and apple sauce. I warn her, I say, what about the flowers? She kisses me on the mouth, her breath tastes peachy keen.

––––––––––

The Order of Things has disappeared, it was right on the bed beside *Paradise Lost*, I was reading apple poems.

I put it on the radio, there beside your damned Harlequin, she says with a shy smile.

I look under the bed. Eye, eye, eye: acres of potato-sized dust-balls, white and fluffy, crying for the shovel.

————————

Dinner by candlelight. Baby passes the apple sauce. The mother pours wine. Borscht bristles with cabbage and onions. Potatoes breathe carbohydrates. We talk about flowers. Frost has my shovel over his shoulder, Foucault fondles the ladder. She walks by a white fishnet, harlequin cap on her head. There is a garden in her face. She nibbles on my ear. The fish leap and leap.

————————

Riddle

Shovel, she says, he shovels the puck into the corner, and we know what she means. But what happens when you shove a story out of bounds or when the story shoves you, propels you forward at a speed faster than you thought possible. You lose track of time, you travel all over the northern hemisphere, search for the golden puck, the Holy Grail, the perfect hockey game, hit a dead end road in Newfoundland, dream of playing in the Big Rink.

Here's the point. She could say a story is like a hockey stick or a shovel or a pencil or a goblet or a computer or a kazoo. They're all the same. They don't do anything unless you do. You play upon a shovel, hockey stick, story, goblet, pencil or computer and they work for you. You can write your name, say, in the snow or use a stick to knock berries from the mountain ash, blood red into the banked drifts, paddle a canoe or a ladder, or stir the leaves, with giant half circles sweep them into bags and bags of backyard piles, or you can warm your hands over the computer, keyboard and wait for the writing and the spring playoffs when the story shoves you into new places, tight corners, rides you/writes you through the summer and into the leaves, slam bang into the clean white snows of December.

The Hockey Fan Dons the Blades Again

1   On Boxing Day I skate on the outdoor rink with Shannon and Andrea, so warm we don't go into the shack but lace up on a picnic bench outside. Shannon and I teach Andrea to play ringette. I tell the girls how we skated on that lake, my brothers and sisters, our rink on the lake by the garden, banks of snow piled high around the fire. They try the stories on for size. Andrea wrinkles her nose and eyes against the sun. Shannon tells me to shush. Her eyes speak of ski hills in the Rockies, of Sunshine and Lake Louise, Fortress Mountain and Nakiska.

2   We get ready for the ringette game. Shannon and I coach the performance. Andrea hauls out her gear: padded collar with velcro fastener, Shannon's nine-year-old ringette jacket, a Boston Bruin sweater handed down from Denis – 12 1/2 years after he first wore it. Her new skates, moulded plastic hockey skates, no picks at the front, soft felt liners to keep her piggies warm. Little red shin guards – the catalogue days are gone – the pads that Denis wore and Mark wore three years before him. Mark and I dragged out of bed in 5:30 Winnipeg mornings to creak the car toward outdoor rinks and pucks frozen hard as coal, ready for anything. Those days are in the family album, catalogued neatly by year and place, as if time and space can be stuck to a page. Mark and Denis stand equipped before the Christmas tree. They are helmeted with their mother's cooking pots, brooms and mops for sticks. They dream of Santa, hope for the gifts, their sisters in the future. That same Christmas Mark, so proud of his new equipment, cracks his jock with his knuckles, so proud, "Grandpa," he says, "Grandpa, I have new shin pads," crack, crack.

I stretch and lace up my skates. Shannon helps Andrea to tug the jill up over her waist, tells how in the old days she didn't wear a jill, only boys wore those things. Andrea tells her to shush.

Jack and Jill

An old Norse story tells how Jack and Jill can be seen in the face of the moon, how Jack's smile makes moonlight for evening skaters and skiers, how Jill's voice echoes in the singing wind. In the Norse story.

The Pastoral Tradition

The kids on defence stand back close to the goalie, lift their sticks into the air and tilt heads back to catch snowflakes on the tongue.

At the other end bundled-up skaters, their wooly scarves flying, flock around the puck.

Stories That Didn't Make It

The neat eyebrows of the shifting Aurora, her hardhat speckled with snow, how her eyes glint and shine, and the Ghadafi story, how his book emblazoned on the chests of his German hockey team got him kicked out of the league. He bought the team and the league said owners are not allowed to advertise books on their uniforms, the writing did him in, the writing on the sweater was the straw that broke the camel's back, they read the writing on the sweater and did him in. The power of writing, riding the sweaters. And how Denis brought a clutch of goblets back from Czechoslovakia. He found four of them, hauled them home in his carry-on, bohemian grails. He got here not long after he had pulled the old peanut-butter-on-the-telephone-receiver trick. The neat row of grails lined up in the china cabinet, their wink and twinkle.

The Hockey Fan Flies Again

Air Canada back and forth, Calgary to Toronto to St. John's. Norcan Air, Saskatoon to Regina, snowing. United Airlines, Calgary to Spokane to Denver, en route to Lincoln Nebraska. *Vis a Vis* the cover says, Bringing You and the World Together. Bold letters over her shoulder, "Defamiliarization" at 30,000 feet over the Rockies, some of the world's most beautiful country says the pilot, Tina Turner on the cover. "Now that advertising has made your product among the best known it may be time to make it strange again."

He skates on the moving sidewalk at Denver Stapleton, hipchecked by his bags (Scotch tucked tight in the corner). Into Lincoln, scouring the local newspapers for hockey news. The NHL scores in a little box tucked into the deepest corner of the sports page. Outside service stations, huge signs predict the score in the next Cornhusker game. A single CNR boxcar parked beside the newspaper building. The next day by bus to Red Cloud. There is no hockey rink in Red Cloud.

To Flin Flon, north and east by Pacific North West he flies, not an ocean in sight. The lakes sparkle in the sun, wait for the chilling frost, for the ice to make.

Overtime

The letters of this story compose themselves in tidy lanes and skate across the page, they glide from gutter to margin and margin to gutter, run down the rivers of the page and turn with leaves in spring and fall. They turn, you turn, I turn. The characters stop and start across the icy page and back again, they become the rhythm of skating and reading and writing. We ride these characters into a life sentence that turns through childhood to youth and middle age, a sentence that stretches until the buzzer sounds and he and she and you and I are bodychecked *belly up belly up* and found wanting.

> *All go tender*
> *All go quick*
> *All jump over*
> *the goalie stick*
> *Go All Go*
> *Go All Go*
> *Go All Go*

He retires three times. The first at the age of 21, when he has a choice: play with the Border Kings and skate along the 49th parallel, or coach the girls' basketball team at the high school where he teaches. Duty calls him.

He retires again when the Big Belly NHL team asks him to turn in his hockey sweater. He hasn't played for a year and they have the gall to ask him to turn in number 9. They go to his house to collect. But it is an anticlimax. Even before that knock on the door his favourite skates are sold right out from under him. Tangible and odorous proof of a glorious hockey career – gone just like that.

So he finds himself on a plane to Europe, retires for a third time, and comes back to earth a middle-aged hockey fan. He begins to compose himself and make another beginning. If you compose yourself and stay on your feet you can fly. On that lakeside rink Gwen and Carol coached him, they said stay on your feet. Don't fall, that's one trip you don't need. If you stay quick on your feet you can fly, you can fly. And of course you fall and scramble to get yourself together and yes you fly, yes you do.